a very no strings halloween

KAYLEY LORING
CONNOR CRAIS

a very no strings
halloween

USA TODAY BESTSELLING AUTHOR
Kayley Loring
Connor Crais

Special Edition Cover Design and Illustrations: Qamber Designs
Copy Editing: Mandi Andrejka, Inky Pen Editing
Proofreading: CM Wheary Editing

For Kayley's mom,
who would have absolutely loved
Billy Boston.

billy

"Here's to you, at ninety years, you old devil," my cousin Nolan says, his whiskey glass raised in a toast to our grandad. "May your joys continue to be as deep as the Irish Sea and your troubles as light as its foam. And may your bloody foot stop givin' you hell, wherever you may roam. Happiest of birthdays to ya, Grandad. Cheers to you, Granny." He gives our eighty-nine-year-old granny a little wink, and she giggles and blushes.

Fucking Irishmen. Guy gets away with everything, and I get smacked upside the head every time I open my mouth since I was old enough to talk. Whatever. He's my best friend, so he gets a pass. I watch as Nolan and his wife, Cora, and their two kids go over to give Grandad hugs. Granny's face just lights up whenever she sees her great-grandkids. It's a beautiful thing.

"Thank you for travelin' from New York, you with your busy lives," Grandad says to them, tapping at his own heart. "Means the world."

Then my cousin Declan gets up to give his toast. Declan's a lawyer in New York and a handsome moth-erfucker in a suit, so all eyes are on him now. He's got his arm around his wife, Maddie, who's holding their baby, Ciara. Then his little brother, Eddie, and his wife, Birdie, from LA, get up. Both of those Cannavale guys with their dueling fake Irish accents. Eddie's an actor, so truth be told, his is a little better—but everyone in this place has stars and shamrocks in their eyes just 'cause these guys do Irish accents.

What the fuck is wrong with a Boston accent, huh?

Why doesn't anyone appreciate the guy who's always around when you need him?

Where is the gratitude for Billy?

There is so much love in this room. It's beautiful. Honest to God, my heart is so full of love for everyone in this big, cluttered pub that's decorated for drunk Irish soccer fans all year long and for Halloween in October and half of November. There's a six-foot animatronic psycho clown thing they bring out every year that's creepy as shit.

But the scariest thing about this room is how much I'm thinking about a certain someone who isn't even in it.

And the second scariest thing about this room

right now is the fact that *none* of the love that's circulating around it is aimed at me.

I'm the guy who rented out my family's favorite Irish pub for the night and invited everyone Granny and Grandad O'Sullivan doesn't hate, from second cousins in Toronto to my pop's old babysitter in Dorchester. I'm the one who flew Nolan's parents and his brothers here to Boston from Ireland. Grandad didn't want me to fly his brothers out, though. "Feck 'em," Grandad said. "I'll see them in hell when we're dead." But *forty* people I flew out to Boston from around North America—on *my* dime. Forty. Has anyone toasted to me yet tonight? Nay, they have not.

Why?

'Cause I'm the only single man left in this entire O'Sullivan clan. From the Cassidys and the Cannavales to the Donovans from Rhode Island. I'm the only bachelor left, hence I must not be responsible and thus worthy of thanks. Doesn't matter that I won the lottery and quadrupled my winnings in investments over the past two years. Doesn't matter that all their kids love me or that I make the best sandwiches anyone has ever tasted. Does anyone remember that I brought the entire room to tears with Neil Diamond's "Play Me" at karaoke night during our last family reunion? Or that I'm the only guy who personally handwrites Christmas cards to everyone in our entire

3

extended family on every continent every year? Nay. They do not.

You set off one firecracker in one toilet at one Thanksgiving dinner when you're twelve and you're labeled the troublemaker for life. It's been, like, five years since I blew anything up. Not counting the thing that happened at the water park that time because it was not on purpose and was not my fault.

This is horseshit is what this is. When my brother, Mark, finally wraps up his long, boring speech and his family goes over to pay their respects to Grandad, I get up on the little stage and take the mic off the stand. Time to show these cocksuckers how it's done.

"Yeah, Mark, it *is* interesting to know all the historical events that were happening around the world when Grandad was born. Wicked interesting." Do I sound like I mean it? I'm doing my best despite being lulled into a coma from his speech. "But it's not just how long you live—it's how much life you live in those years that counts. Am I right? The O'Sullivan clan has always had, shall we say, an adventurous streak. It's what inspired Grandad to cross an ocean with his bride and settle in this country for a fresh start. It's what gave him the stones to ask Granny for a date in front of her parents when she was fifteen."

There's some rustling in the crowd. What? Not like I said *gonads* or *wank tanks*. I used the classy term.

"One of my favorite stories about Grandad is the time my pops got interested in hot-air balloons. Because not only are the O'Sullivans adventurous, fun, and dedicated to livin' life to the fullest—we *nevah* do anything halfway. Grandad could've read him stuff from some boring book like Mark just did." I gesture toward my brother, who does not look pleased. But he looks displeased fully, with his whole heart and soul and face, like a true O'Sullivan. "No, Grandad didn't do that. He spent weeks in the backyard with my dad buildin' a hot-air balloon. Because that's the other thing about O'Sullivans...we're very good with our hands."

I waggle my eyebrows for effect. But lest I be accused of being unable to read a room, I drop it. Tough crowd.

"Sure, my grandad let Pops go up in the hot-air balloon alone. Should he have used a stronger rope to tether it to the ground? Mark's boring historians would most likely say yes. Did the rope snap? It did. Did nine-year-old Oscar O'Sullivan float off over the streets of Boston for an hour? He did indeed. But did Grandad chase after him the entire way, never taking his eyes off him? Fuck yeah, he did. Even while being repeatedly whacked in the back of the head by my granny's purse. Even as she screamed at him to get their son down—so loudly, legend has it, that Irish American fathers from South Boston all the way to

Worcester were frantically looking up, trying to find their sons so they could retrieve them from the sky.

"Pops learned about hot-air balloons and the need for strong ropes to match the forces of drag and wind shear. He learned all that in a way my brother's boring books could never teach anyone—the absolute terror of being trapped in a runaway hot-air balloon. But Pops didn't just learn—he lived. Thanks to Grandad. So here's to ninety years of living life to the fullest! *Sláinte!*"

Mic drop.

And here come the cheers.

More for Grandad than for me, but it's cool.

I just wish a certain someone could have heard that story. She would have appreciated it. But that is neither here nor there. Because she'd never want to be here.

I take my seat at the table again, and my dad shakes his head at me. Half frowning, half grinning, in that way of his. You can never tell if he's amazed by your awesomeness or your stupidity until he either pats you on the back so hard you feel the palm of his appreciative hand there for an hour or he smacks you up the side of the head. "You had to tell 'em the hot-air balloon story."

"It's a wicked good story."

He smacks me up the side of the head.

"What?! People loved it!"

My grandad grabs his glass of Guinness and stands up at his table. For an old guy, he's still got a booming yet somehow melodic voice. "Thank you. From the bottom of me heart, I thank all of you. After livin' the near century that I have lived, you do, indeed, learn a thing or two along the way. But alas, when you live long enough, you also start forgettin' many of those things. Which is why it's important to meet a person. And to make that person your family." My grandad looks lovingly at my granny. She absolutely beams up at him. Their skin is wrinkled as a nut sac that's been boiling in a hot tub for too long, but the look in their eyes makes them seem seventy years younger.

"And then you gotta make more people with 'em..." Grandad continues suggestively. People laugh at him, totally charmed by him. He didn't even have to waggle his eyebrows. Granny giggles and blushes again. *Because Irish accent.* "So that those people you make can grow up and find their people and make them family." My grandad looks over at Pops and Ma, his eyes slick and shiny with pride. "So they can make more people to meet people and make more family." He glances at Mark and my cousins and all of his grandchildren. Somehow he's able to scan the entire room while overlooking me. It's actually pretty impressive. "And so on and so forth, so that a long life becomes fuller the longer you go. And these people in your family can teach you the lessons and remind you what's important every single day when you live so long that you start to forget. And aye, adventure is grand. But all adventure stories reach a final page. 'Tis love and family that brings immortality. So here's to lovin' and livin' forever." He raises his glass and everyone follows suit.

It was a good speech. Mine was objectively more fun. But no word of thanks about me organizing this here party. For getting everyone here. For delivering a kick-ass speech after Mark nearly bored everyone to death.

Grandad clears his throat and fixes me with his dark-eyed stare. Here we go. He didn't forget. He was just saving the best for last. "So, what are we gonna do with this one? Heh? Billy, my boy, *when* are ya finally gonna find someone? When are you gonna find a nice lass to make you immortal?"

"When he finds one that's blind, deaf, *and* a Tomcats fan!" Nolan shouts out.

Oh yeah, that gets a big laugh.

Let's all laugh at Billy Boston for being single and wicked awesome!

"Maybe when I fly to Vegas and find one drunk enough to accidentally marry me!"

Record scratch. Seriously. The one second there isn't a Dropkick Murphys song blaring from the speakers. That does not get the response I was hoping for. Possibly because most of the people here aren't supposed to know about how Nolan and Cora woke up married in Vegas. From the look Nolan's giving me, I'd say I might not live to see my next birthday.

Moving on.

"Hey! Another round of drinks on me!" I shout, to everyone in particular. Literally all of the drinks have been on me tonight, but that's the one sentence I can yell out at this gathering that guarantees me a positive response.

"What're we gonna do with you, though, William?"

Uh-oh.

I turn to find my ma resting her chin on her fist. Her elbow slips off the edge of the table, but she straightens herself up and then refolds the napkin in her lap, like she did that on purpose. She only calls me William after she's had three glasses of pinot grigio. Four and she starts picking fights with Granny, and five... I shudder at the very thought. We cannot allow her to get to five.

Ma's from New Jersey. She's been living in Boston for, like, thirty-five years, but nobody here understands what she's saying half the time. But they can hear her! When I was ten she woke us all up in the middle of the night, screaming from down the hall: *Billy, you get down from there right now! This is very bad for my heart—you get down from there! Gimme a kiss, baby, that's my good boy.* She was fast asleep. Pops says she still wakes him up by dream-yelling at me a few nights a year. Usually after someone in our family gets married.

"Come over here, sweetie! I love you—look at this face—will you look at this handsome face on my boy?!" she exclaims to no one in particular. "I love this face—but how are you gonna meet someone special if you're always gallivantin' around town, huh?"

"My point exactly," my aunt Mamie says. Mrs. Cannavale is the unspoken boss of everyone in the entire family, and my ma's fine with it since she can only give so many fucks about so many people.

"Come 'ere. Give your ma a kiss." She holds her arms out toward me.

"Maaaaa. Come on."

"Not on the lips—calm down, *mistah*. C'mere to your ma who loves you!"

I do. I give my ma a kiss on the cheek. She tries to slick back my wavy hair, but I step away from her. "Maaa."

"It's gettin' too long in the back!"

"It's, like, half an inch below my earlobe!"

"Come back to the house and lemme trim it for you! You think I don't know what's right for my boy?"

"Ma. I swear to God. Not now."

"Leah! Leah!" Suddenly she's yelling at the waitress and waving her over. "Leah, what do you think? You think my son could use a trim?"

Jesus Christ.

Leah's carrying two trays of pint glasses, and she looks at me like she wants to throw all of them in my face.

"I got no idea what your son needs, Mrs. O'Sullivan, besides better manners." She turns on her heel and walks away.

"What the fuck is her problem?" my ma rightfully asks. "Billy, did you mess with her already?"

"I mean..." Did I hang out with the cute waitress from my favorite pub a couple of times a few years ago? Yeah. Did she overreact when she asked me to drive her to a medical appointment wherein she was going to have the fat removed from her ass and injected into her lips, and I told her to leave the fat where it was? Yeah, in my humble opinion, she did. By that time it was clear we were trying to find love and fat in all the wrong places. "It wasn't a good fit, all right?"

"I do not like her attitude. Who does she think she is, talkin' to me like that about my son?"

"Right?"

"She's too blonde for you anyway," Mrs. C says. "I don't see you with a blonde. We met a nice girl on the plane yesterday...what was her name? Nice, strong personality, very polite. What was her name? Tony—what was that girl's name who sat on the other side of the aisle from us yesterday?" Her husband is in the middle of a conversation with my dad. I don't see that it matters what this girl's name was since she isn't here and they obviously didn't get her number. "Tony. Tony! Tony!"

"What?!"

"What was the name of that girl across the aisle from us?"

He looks around, exasperated. "What aisle?"

"On the plane! Yesterday! The one I said would be good for Billy."

Mr. C shrugs. "Patricia. Why does it matter what her name was? She lives in Cleveland and we didn't get her number."

"Patty!" Mamie ignores her husband as soon as he gives her the name. "That's the kind of girl you should settle down with, Billy. She had red hair. That's what you need. A redhead." She nods, like this is the wisest thing anyone will ever say to me.

And maybe it is. I do like redheads. Or *a* redhead.

But that's irrelevant. "Sounds good, Mrs. C. I'm gonna go talk to Dec." I raise my hand and nod at Declan, as if he's been trying to get my attention. He hasn't. But I need to get out of this situation.

And just when I'm trying, as always, not to think about a certain redhead that I can't seem to stop thinking about, my phone vibrates with a text notification.

Red: *You home?*

And suddenly, the clouds part and bright red sun shines through.

Me: *I am at home in the world, Red. You know that. I'll be back at my apartment later. You at home?*
Red: *Affirmative.*
Me: *And you're dying to see me. Well, well. What are we gonna do about that?*
Red: *I have ideas, Mouth. But first you need to get over yourself.*
Me: *I think we both know that's never gonna happen. Hope the rest of your ideas involve getting under me.*

"Who are you texting with?"

If anyone else had said anything to me just now, I'm quite sure I wouldn't have heard them. But it's Maddie. And she's smiling. So I will answer her.

Sliding my phone back into my pocket, I say, "Ah, y'know."

"Well, I *don't* know, Billy. That's why I'm asking. You seem awfully happy to be communicating with whoever it is."

"Nawww." That can't be right. Horny, maybe. My dick is happy all of a sudden—for Red reasons. Not because my cousin's wife is talking to me. "You guys havin' a good night?" I ask, swiftly changing the subject. "Can I get you something from the bar?"

"No, I'm good. Tonight has been a blast. Thank you for organizing this, Billy," she says as she holds her toddler, Ciara, up. "You want to take her for a bit?"

"Hell yeah, I do. Hey, kid." I hoist up the little princess in the crook of my arm. It's been way too long since they asked me to fly out and babysit her. "How's my girl doin'? You sleepy?"

She nods, slow-blinking at me. "Yeah."

"Yeah, me too. Let's take a nap right now." I shut my eyes and snore loudly.

Finally, I'm getting the laughs I deserve. Twinkling, tired-little-girl toddler laughs.

I open my eyes again and wink at her. "Ahhh. That was refreshin'."

"Thanks again for organizing this," Dec chimes in. As if he's already thanked me and now he's thanking me again. "I'll take her." He gets up from his chair to take his daughter from me. Poor jealous guy can't handle how much his kid loves me.

"Ohhh, okay. Let's let your daddy hold you, Little C."

Ciara immediately starts pouting and then slow-motion erupts into a crying fit as he pulls her into his arms. Poor Manhattan. I'd feel bad for the guy if he weren't a rich, handsome lawyer with a beautiful wife and child.

His beautiful wife pats my arm. "Ohhh, Billy! That reminds me. Are you going to be in town in a couple of weeks?"

"*Maddie*," Declan mutters. "No."

Maddie waves him off. "Are you? Middle of October?"

"Yeah, I can be. Why?"

"My niece Piper is dying to go to a book signing event at Harvard. You remember Piper."

"Yeah, yeah. Cute kid. What is she, twelve?"

"She'll be graduating from high school next year, actually."

"Fuck me, that's insane." I cover my mouth. "Sorry."

Dec narrows his eyes at me, but Maddie doesn't care.

"No, I know. It is insane. But her favorite author is doing a thing hosted by the Harvard Book Store, and I guess this woman refuses to even go to New York because she's a huge Boston Tomcats fan—"

"*Undahstandable*."

"So Piper got a ticket, but both of her parents are busy that weekend, and Dec and I are too. It's just for the day—she's planning to take the train."

"It would be my honor to be her chaperone. I'll pay for her flight. Pick her up at the airport."

"That is not happening," Dec assures us.

"That would make her so happy!" Maddie

exclaims, clapping her hands, all tipsy and ignoring her husband. "I'm pretty sure my sister will be okay with this because she's still trying to get Piper to think she's cool."

"Not happening," Dec calmly reiterates.

"I'll help you draft a contract for both of them to sign," Maddie tells Declan, winking at me with her back to him and mouthing, *No, I won't.*

Behind her back, Dec mouths to me, *I will fucking murder you if anything happens to her.*

"You got it," I say to both of them. "I'll take good care of her."

"This is highly problematic," my cousin says to Maddie. "You realize that, right?"

My phone keeps buzzing in my back pocket.

All of my attention is now focused on my right ass cheek.

I can just sense her texts in there. That saucy little minx. What kind of ideas do you have for us tonight, huh, Red?

I reach for my phone but freeze as soon as I hear my best friend's threatening tone.

"Well, if it ain't Mr. Bigmouth Chucklehead Fuckup Magee…"

My cousin Nolan has two speeds—threatening you with a good time and just plain threatening you. He's a family man now, so the former happens a lot less than the latter, unfortunately.

"What? You don't want people to know the beginning of your beautiful love story?"

"I just spent the last ten minutes explaining to Granny that poor, confused, wayward Billy was mistaken and it was, in fact, only me who was wildly drunk in Vegas, not the wonderful mother of my children." Nolan puts a protective, loving arm around Cora as punctuation. She smiles at me, conveying that she appreciates the gesture but she doesn't think it's such a big deal. Cora's good people. "Granny found that very believable," Nolan says.

"That you were drunk?" I ask with a grin that eats all the shit.

"That you were confused. And lost."

That's it. I've had enough of this. "Oh yeah? I wasn't too confused and lost to make this entire party happen without any help from anyone!"

"I think what Nolan was trying to say," Cora tells me, her tone reprimanding her husband to stop giving me shit, "is that he just wants you to be as happy as he is."

"Aye. Exactly that, *macushla*." Nolan pulls her closer and kisses the top of her forehead. The fuckhead really does seem happy. Not in the way that I'm happy. His happiness now comes from a deep well. Nolan looks back at me. "But alas, dear Billy's not built for it. He wouldn't be able to get a real girlfriend if the Tomcats' season depended on it."

I narrow my eyes at him. "*Mothahfucka*, I could get a serious girlfriend if I wanted to—easy. Seven days a week and twice on Sunday."

"Ya could not."

"Could too."

"Could not."

"Could too!"

This is how it's gone with us for about twenty-five years. It's how I ended up in a hotel pool from five stories up. It's how we both ended up driving a golf cart on the side of the highway while on a mission to get lobster rolls. It's how I ended up becoming a beekeeper for an entire summer between sophomore and junior year.

The only difference now is that Cora is here to roll her eyes at us. And that I'm older. Wiser. Not as easily manipulated.

"Don't bother, Nolan. You're never going to get him to cave," Eddie butts in.

Like I was born yesterday.

Nice try, Eddie. Too old. Too fuckin' wise. Not gonna take the bait.

Nolan grins, a grin that threatens a good time for him and a wicked bad one for me. "You're right, Eddie. He's just. Too. Chicken."

"That's it, *cocksucka*—you're on!" I yell, pointing a finger in Nolan's face.

"Shall we wager a bet, then?" Nolan asks with an

evil smirk that tells me the asshole had something in mind since before he walked over here. "A bet that says you won't have a verified serious girlfriend by the time we're all back here celebratin' Granny's ninetieth in November. And none of this fake-girlfriend malarkey Declan pulled with Maddie either."

"Hey," Declan snaps. "It was only fake for a couple of weeks."

"Nolan," Cora reprimands. "Don't be mean."

"If you lose this bet, you wear New York Rebels gear, head to toe, at a game where the Tomcats face the Rebels. And you will post pictures of yourself in said clothing on all of your social media."

"You devious bastard. How dare you."

"And if by some miracle you do, in fact, bring us a woman who is genuinely committed to being in a monogamous relationship with you, *I* will dress head to toe in Boston Tomcats gear at a game, even though they play the wrong kind of football."

"I'll take that action," Eddie says. "If Billy wins, I will also wear Boston Tomcats gear in public and post pics of myself wearing said gear on my social media."

That handsome little fuck. "You don't give a shit one way or another whose team you're wearin'. That doesn't mean anythin'. It's gotta have teeth, or you aren't a part of this."

"I have an idea!" Eddie's adorable wife, Birdie, appears and chimes in. "If Billy wins, Eddie will wear

Benedict-Cumberbatch-as-Sherlock fan merch in public for one week."

His very impressive jaw clenches, even though he's smiling at his little blonde bride. "What? That wouldn't bother me at all, babe."

"You're on. That is happening."

Eddie frowns at me.

"You poor, stupid fucks," I say to Nolan and Eddie. "I'm gonna have a relationship so stable you could keep horses in it."

"We'll see, Billy Boyo. We'll see," says Nolan.

My phone pings again, and I walk away from Nolan and Eddie, giving them the Boston Salute as I go.

I finally take my phone out and open up my text messages.

Red: Well, if you happen to know a good pipe jockey, I've got some plumbing that needs to be fixed ASAP ;)
Red: It needs to be fixed real bad.
Red: And by "bad" I mean hard and fast.
Red: Let me know.

Yeah, I gotta bounce. In honor of my grandad, I do it in the manner of my ancestors. I go full Irish goodbye and say sayonara to no one as I blow this hole to go lay some pipe.

donna

THE CAULKING DREAD

Mouth: *Plumber is on his way to you. Wants to know if he should bring a drain snake or a caulk gun. Please advise.*

That's cute. I step into the leopard-print lace trim lingerie that I bought four years ago and haven't worn since I started stress-eating my feelings. Or since I ate those two bags of fun-size Halloween candy that I got on sale in early September and drank all that beer for Oktoberfest. *Here goes nothing...* Inhaling, I lift the slip by its dainty little silk straps, but...it doesn't want to slide up past my badonkadonk.

So close!

I can do this.

I *will* do this.

I am trying to pull the stupid, frigging beautiful, delicate slip over my head and past my giant boobs when my phone starts playing the opening of Michael Jackson's "Thriller." It's been my ringtone for a week, and it still freaks me out and cracks me up every time I hear it. Carefully reaching out to accept the call without tearing the seams of the nightie, I yell out, "After the week I've had, I need caulk *and* a snake! Give me five minutes!"

"*Ach du lieber Gott, Mädchen!*" comes the voice of my seventy-nine-year-old grandmother.

"Ohhhh heeeyyyy, Oma! Hang on a second!"

"What is going on over there?! Why does it sound like your boobs are squished?"

Sucking everything in, I pull the damn silk down over my boobs and hips with one frantic tug—and I don't hear anything rip apart. The badonkadonk is adequately covered. It looks like my boobs are trying to hug my neck, but it'll have to do. I just won't be able to sit or breathe while I'm wearing this. I touch the speakerphone icon. "Sorry about that, Oma! Just got back from my shift, so I'm changing my clothes!"

"Whose cock is giving you only five minutes, *Püppchen*?" she asks, genuinely distraught. "You had better get a lot of foreplay! This is exactly why I am calling you. Why do you not have a proper boyfriend again to take care of you? Come back to Philadelphia, Donna. Let me help you find a man who treats you right. The men in Boston *schtink*!"

"Yah. Like their sports teams!" My opa calls out in the background.

I want to laugh, but I can't because my boobs are squished. "Oh, hey, Opa. I'm just waiting for a plumber to come over." My grandparents are my favorite people, but I refuse to talk cock with them, no matter how much my oma sounds like Dr. Ruth. And I definitely don't want to have the *why don't I have a proper boyfriend* conversation.

"What is so bad you have to pay for a plumber at this hour?" My grandfather's voice is so loud and deep on the phone, it always sounds like he's mad at me. "Do you have a clog or a leak?"

"Um. Both? It's not exactly an emergency—I just don't feel like taking care of it all by myself tonight." I spritz a musky perfume on my pulse points. Assuming there are pulse points in my cleavage and inner thighs.

"If you have bad plumbing at your apartment, why do you not move to the house?"

Ahhh, the house. A shiver goes down my spine as I think about that huge old farmhouse out in Middleborough. My favorite patient left it to me in a kind act of generosity, and it has so far been nothing but a terrifying ass ache. "Because there are a lot more issues with that house than plumbing. It's an old, old house and a big, big project, Opa. I don't have time to deal with it now."

"Then why not sell the house *und* buy a condo?" he very rightfully asks.

I don't know when would be a good time to tell him that house is possibly haunted and probably unsellable, but it's definitely not now.

There's a cocky knock at my front door. Thank God. I might not be able to stay awake more than five minutes. "Plumber's here—I gotta go! I love you both. Say hi to Mom if you talk to her tomorrow. I probably won't have time!"

"You deserve no less than fifteen minutes of cock, *Püppchen*!" Oma yells as I'm hanging up. "On top of the foreplay!"

More insistent banging on the door, but I can't stop smiling. This guy bangs the way he does everything else—loudly, with urgency and confidence and his whole heart. And big, strong hands.

Fluffing up my hair and pausing to get into character first, I attempt a deep breath—as deep as my silk-imprisoned bosom will allow—and then open the door. The plumber is casually resting one hand against the door frame, holding a big toolbox in his other hand and smirking at me lasciviously. Until his beautiful brown eyes widen and his jaw drops when he takes in all there is to take in of me in this slip dress. His flannel shirt is completely unbuttoned, revealing the dark hair on his chest and abs that in no way reveal all the

Dunkin' Donuts and beer that I am certain he has consumed in his life.

"That's how you dress for work?" I ask, placing my hands on my hips.

"That's how you dress to answer the door in the middle of the night?"

"I didn't have time to change. My homicidally jealous and possessive ex-husband could show up at any minute. We need to—I mean, you need to get to work."

And there's that smirk again. "Oh, I am ready to get to work, Missus—I didn't get your name, sweetheart?"

"*Ms.* Ballcock."

"German, huh?"

"*Yah*. And you are?"

"Rod. Rod Auger. Here's my card." With the flick of his wrist, he produces a business card for an Irish pub. "Other side, sweetheart."

I flip the card over. It just says *1-800-ROD-JOBS*, scrawled in blue ink. I glance up at him. He winks at me. I slip the card into my cleavage for safekeeping, slowly, so Rod can thoroughly enjoy watching me do it. "Thanks, Rod. I'll hold on to this. Come inside." I place my hands on either side of the door frame and lean forward to look down the hall, nervously biting my lip as my boobs press against his warm body. "Better hurry before anyone sees you."

"Ladies first." His voice is low all of a sudden, and I feel it deep and warm in my belly. "No matter how quick and dirty the job gets. Always—ladies first..." He stands totally still as I slowly pull back to meet his gaze. I trust this man, but there's something so exciting about him. I never really know what he's going to say or do. I just know that I've liked everything he's ever said and done to me.

I step back, holding the door open, and check out his butt in those dark jeans as he walks past me. At night, he usually smells like either Guinness or whiskey. Guinness or whiskey plus something else. Guinness and maple syrup. Whiskey and cigar smoke. Guinness and paint. Whiskey and a clean hotel room. Tonight he smells like Guinness and chocolate.

"So, what's the emergency *ovah heah*, Ms. Ballcock?" He kicks off his shoes, leaves them by the door. So considerate. "What do we got? Clog? Pressure issue? Leak?"

"Oh, there is definitely some leakage," I say, squeezing my thighs together. "In the kitchen." I lead him to the kitchen, sashaying because there's no other way to walk in this thing. "It's just *so* wet down there. Very slippery."

"Oh, yeah? How long has this been goin' on?"

"Ever since you knocked on my front door." My kitchen is lit only by the range hood light, and I am not going to turn on the overheads. "It's the dishwasher," I

26

tell him as I attempt to bend over in front of him and pull open the dishwasher door. "Sorry it's such a small kitchen. Tight fit."

He drops his toolbox on the counter with a thud, startling me, but it doesn't startle me nearly as much as the big hard tool in his pants when he quickly, ever so subtly presses it against my ass and gently places his hands on my hips to move me out of the way. "Tight and wet. Oh no, such difficult working conditions. 'Scuse me, ma'am. I need to get in there."

"Hopefully there's something you can do. It's been a while since I've let anyone under the hood. Is that what it's called? The hood?"

"Yeah, sure, why not. D'you run this tonight? Or is this load dirty?"

"It is absolutely filthy."

He presses a button and slams the door shut. "Just the way I like it." The dishwasher cycle starts as his face hovers just above mine. I grip the edge of the counter behind me. "Fixed it." He stares down at my mouth and roughly cups my face with one hand.

"Fix *me* now, Rod," I whisper, clutching at his open shirt, my voice trembling like the rest of me. "Hurry. My terrible, horrible ex could walk through that door any minute."

"Let him. I'm here to fix everything and protect you. I ain't gonna rush this, baby—not the first time." He grunts as the palms of his hands skim my hard nipples beneath the silk. It's heaven the way the fabric feels against my skin, beneath his warm, rough hands. "Goddamn, you are so fucking hot. You feel how hard I am already? You feel that?"

I slide my hand down his abs and over the hard length in his jeans. "Yeah. It feels good. Your tool's so much bigger than my ex-husband's."

"Forget about your ex, baby. By the time I'm done pumpin' and flushin' your pipes, you won't remember his name. I bet my male line's gonna fit your female union *juuuust* right."

"I need you to snake my drain—hurry!" I plead. I am so turned on and so tired.

"What is this, satin?" He slips his hands under the hem and squeezes my ass.

"It's one hundred percent mulberry silk!"

"Sooo silky. Like your tight, drippin'-wet pussy?"

The mouth on this one, I swear. He slowly lowers himself down the front of my body until his knees touch the floor and then swiftly yanks the skirt up past my hips. I close my eyes and thread my fingers through his wavy hair as the tip of his thumb presses against my clit over the mesh thong. I cannot wait to feel his short beard scraping the skin of my inner thighs. "Jesus fuck, baby, you're so wet... Wait...everything's wet. My feet are wet. What the hell?"

It isn't until he stands up again that I realize my feet are wet too. I'm standing in a puddle. "Shit."

billy

"Shit. Shit, not again!" Donna pulls out all the hand towels from a drawer and throws them onto the floor. "Turn off the dishwasher—turn it off!"

I leap over the puddle and hit a button on the washer to turn it off. "Wait, your dishwasher really was leakin'?"

"It did the last time I ran it, yeah." Donna runs to the linen closet in the hallway to grab more towels, or more like shuffles very quickly, because her wicked hot little silky dress thing is so tight.

"Well, why didn't you say so?"

"What do you mean?!" She drops more towels onto the floor to soak up the hot water. "I did."

"But you gotta admit—the outfit, the names, you kinda led with the 'fantasy' part more than the 'my dishwasher needs some actual repairs' part."

Donna lets out a big, stress-filled, exasperated sigh. That shouldn't do anything for me, but it heaves her wonderful rack even higher up out of the top of her tight little dress before it descends gently on the off breath. "Well, that's because I knew I could just *not* run the dishwasher when it's leaking, but it's a lot harder to not have sex when I'm horny!" She looks up at me. We're both still breathing a little heavy and her cheeks are flushed. Both from trying to create a flood in her panties and from preventing a flood in her kitchen.

Sometimes I can't believe she's real. She's the prettiest girl I've ever been with. The lock of hair matted to her forehead from a little sweat somehow only adds to her charm. Everything she does and everything she says only ever *adds*. If they used pictures of her body in geometry textbooks, guys would understand curvature in an instant. Hourglasses get their inspiration from the shape of her body, not the other way around. When the Animaniacs said, *Hellooooooo, nurse!* they were talking to Donna and only to her.

But Donna isn't my girlfriend. We don't date. We role-play and pretend to be other people—people who don't really know each other—because it's fun and it de-stresses her. She gets it. This wonderful, beautiful, fun broad gets it. And I fucking love giving it to her. But I do know her well enough now to see that there's stress in her eyes beneath all that lust. Her panties may be wet, but so are her floors and her appliance is broken. This is a woman who works hard, and she wants the things in her life to work when she needs them to. She's not going to be able to really relax until her dishwasher's fixed. And if she's awake, she's out of the apartment for her job, so she can't wait around during the day.

So I do the hardest thing I think I've done since trying to give up Dunkin' for Lent. I think beyond how hard I am right at this very moment and consider the big picture. "Well, how about I fix it and then we fuck."

"How about we fuck first and then you fix it," Donna replies, pouting and trying to get my arms to wrap around her luscious body again.

"If a fake plumber gets you goin' just wait until you watch me lay pipe for real," I say with a grin that I know is dangerous.

Donna smirks, trying to arm herself against my charm. *Good luck with that, lady.* "Well, as I've already said many times tonight—hurry up, Rod."

I inspect the dishwasher, opening the door. A little more water pours out, and I shut it quickly. "Shouldn't take long at all. Bet it's just a kinked drain hose."

"Well, I think it's unfair the hose gets to be kinky and I'm over here all alone," she pouts again, completely adorable.

"Just have a seat, sweet cheeks, and watch my big strong hands remove this unit."

"I can't sit in this thing." She waves her hand up and down her magnificent lingerie.

"Well, then turn around, put your hands on the wall, and spread your legs." I wink at her. She laughs and shakes her head. Instead, she chooses to fold her arms, pushing her breasts up, and leans one luscious hip against the counter while I get to work.

I take a screwdriver out of my toolbox and start removing the screws that attach the dishwasher unit to the cabinets. "So is it just the dishwasher?"

"What do you mean?"

What do I mean? I'm asking what's going on with her emotionally. In her life. Even though that's against the no-strings rules. When we started this arrangement, it was made clear by both of us that if this had any hope of staying fun, we couldn't burden each other with our real-life problems. Only made-up problems of people like Rod Auger and Ms. Ballcock. Instead of analyzing why I'm asking, I just say, "I dunno. Is there something wrong, or is it just the dishwasher bringing you down?"

"Isn't that breaking the rules?" Donna asks, as if reading my mind.

I pocket the screws and shrug without looking at her, staying focused on the dishwasher. "You're not offering. I'm asking. I think we can get off on a technicality."

She hesitates, and I take that moment to pull the dishwasher out. It covers whatever awkward pause was about to happen between us with the scraping of metal against linoleum. Which I prefer, for some reason. Would it hurt if she says no? That's ridiculous. That's literally her business. When the dishwasher is out far enough so I can see the back and the connecting drain hose, the quiet returns. And I just wait to see if she wants to fill it with an answer.

"I had a tough day at work."

"Oh yeah?" I don't look at her. I focus on the drain hose, which is indeed kinked and not installed properly. Because I think if I look at her, she'll stop talking.

"Yeah. No one died. Which as you know, in my line of work, happens."

"Yeah," I say, because I don't know what else to say. Her job as a private nurse is incredibly important and incredibly heavy and something I know I wouldn't be able to do.

"It was just a miscommunication with someone who was supposed to come to my patient's house today to help me with something, so I had to do it myself. It was a scheduling conflict that's falling on me. And it's not a big deal. It wasn't a life-or-death situation, which makes me feel even dumber about being so annoyed by it."

"Well, you can only ever have your problems. Even if they're not life or death. They're still yours, and there's still a problem." I look up at her when she doesn't say anything. She's looking at me with a strange look on her face. "What?"

"That's pretty wise, Billy Boston."

"I'm full of wisdom, Donna Fischer." With a smile that confirms I know just how full of wisdom and charm I am.

"You're full of something," she says with a laugh.

The hose is unkinked and the unit is draining again. I start working on hooking the hose in the proper place. "You sound like my cousins."

Donna sighs again. "Well, that's the other thing— relatives. My oma was bugging me about dating again. People just don't get why it's awesome to not be tied down. Because even though you're wise, Billy, you're also wrong. I *can* have the problems of Ms. Ballcock, who has a jealous ex-husband and the need to be fucked by her sexy plumber."

"Sexy, *wise* plumber," I correct her. I hook the drain hose onto the back and push the dishwasher under the countertop. "Well, I don't know about the rest, but this'll be one less problem Donna Fischer has to worry about."

"Is it done already?"

"Almost," I say, rotating the screws back in. "I had

a similar situation, I guess. Though I'm not supposed to be sharing, am I?"

"I'll allow it," she says, waving her hand in the air like a queen. That sounds like a fun scenario for later. I shall serve her and be queened by a queen.

I take a deep breath. *Come on, Billy, you're a fake professional plumber. Focus.* "So, I was at this family thing, right? And everyone's giving me shit about still being single. The usual crap. My cousin Nolan, the one who knows I'm completely full of wisdom, even bet me I couldn't find a serious girlfriend by November."

Red snorts. "That's stupid."

"Tell me about it," I grumble, tightening a screw with maybe a bit more force than is necessary. Especially because I'm starting to feel confused about which part of that is stupid. The fact that they think I should have one, the fact that they think I can't get one, or the fact that I don't have one.

"So is Halloween the deadline, then?"

"Yeah, I suppose it is."

"I've got Halloween off this year for a change. Gonna hand out candy to the trick-or-treaters in the building. You're welcome to join me. Contribute some Mounds bars to the cause if you don't have a girl by then."

"Thanks, but I've got this big Halloween party I'm supposed to hit." I almost tell her that if I don't have a girlfriend by then, Halloween is when I'm guaranteed to wake up next to one the day after. Most people find hookups during Halloween. They go out at night, pretend to be other people, get shit-faced, and have a good time. They leave their inhibitions at home for a change. But getting shit-faced and having a good time is my life. Those Halloween partiers are tourists visiting my home country. And on nights like that, the *real* Billy Boston seems like boyfriend material.

"Well, great. More candy for me, then." She sounds disappointed, though. Which is strange. I must be imagining things. But we both lapse into silence as I focus on the dishwasher. I run a quick cycle, and everything seems to be working properly.

"She's draining and running smoothly now," I announce proudly. "Now, are you ready to..." My mouth snaps shut when I look over at Donna. Her eyes are closed. Not in a *I'm so turned on by Billy's real-life plumbing skills that I'm going to give Rod's rod the ride of his life and I need to shut my eyes for a moment to contain my pleasure* kind of shut-eye. They're *I'm so exhausted that I fell asleep standing up* closed.

"Donna?" I say gently.

Her eyes pop wide open in a flash. "What? I'm here. Let's do it."

Laughing, I shake my head. Donna is a pretty great actress. I mean, even if she wasn't I'd have a blast role-playing with her. She's really good at it. But she's completely full of shit right now. "Nah, you're beat.

You should go to sleep," I tell her, even though a part of me—a very hard, frustrated part—is screaming to take her up on her offer.

"I just need a quick little nap," she mumbles, moving to her bedroom and flopping down onto the bed. She curls up into a little ball, and the seams of her silk cheetah-or-whatever lingerie rips. I sigh, because I should have been the one to rip that off her. She doesn't even seem to notice that it's torn. She looks so vulnerable now. She still looks really fucking sexy, but it morphs into something else. Something more. Something beautiful. "Five minutes, I promise," she says sleepily.

"Five minutes," I say, playing along. "And then I'll ravish you before your jealous ex gets here."

"Yeah, five minutes before my drain gets plugged..." she slurs, already half asleep.

Her bed is perfectly made, and she's on top of it. I look around, finding a folded blanket on the seat of an armchair. I gently spread it over her and tuck her in with my large hands that should be gripping her and vigorously massaging things by now. Part of me wants to curl up with her, to feel her warmth against me, to wake up next to her in the morning. But that's against the rules too.

I never stay the night. Those are the rules. No catching feelings. If either of us ever starts to get serious about the other or wants more than sex, we have to end it. We made a pact.

I kiss her forehead, inhaling the citrus scent of her shampoo. "Night, Red."

She responds with the heavy, slow breathing of a deep, much-needed sleep.

I pick up my boots and let myself out of her apartment, making sure I lock the door on my way out. Thankfully it's not a long commute back to my place. Only a few steps right next door.

I take a deep breath. I'm frustrated. And confused. And horny. And maybe a little pissed? Why am I feeling all these things? I know why. There's only one person who's making me feel this way.

Nolan.

Fucking Nolan.

Me: *Hey, Shitbag. Let's go get wasted.*
Fucking Nolan: *Wish I could, but my daughter is having trouble sleeping. She needs me. Another night, you fuck.*

Well, I need you too, I think to myself. *I need you to get shit-faced with me. Do I not count at all anymore?*

Me: *Dec. Drinks. Now. Meet me in the bar at your hotel in half an hour or I will come find you.*
Manhattan: *The answer is no. Even if it weren't Sunday night, it would be no. And if you show up*

here and wake up my sleeping child I will destroy you. Or bury what's left of you after Maddie gets to you first.
Manhattan: *But thanks again for organizing Grandad's party.*

Well, that is not ideal. Seems pretty out of bounds to use your cute children against your cousin. And Dec and Nolan know I won't do what I used to do, which is show up at their residences to party by force. And I know not to disturb Eddie because Pretty Boy needs his beauty sleep for some big movie he's getting ready for.

The good ol' days are really over, I guess.

I take off my wet socks and climb into bed with my clothes still on, staring at the wall next to me. Donna's right on the other side of it. For a brief moment I picture that wall demolished. Then I shake my head and laugh.

Walls are good. Walls keep things fun and not messy. Walls keep you from getting tangled up and strangled by strings.

No strings. That's the way to go.

Nolan and Dec and Eddie and my ma and Aunt Mamie and Grandad are all wrong. I have already secured my immortality. People know me by reputation. By my deeds and the epic tales of my debauchery. I don't need a girlfriend.

Donna gets it. She's fun. And funny. And bright. And beautiful.

But she knows that serious relationships just keep you down. Serious relationships bring down the entire party that is life.

I don't *need* a girlfriend. But I'll get one to win a bet. That's it.

All I need is Donna.

Who I can't have right now. Because she's on that side of the wall and I'm on this one. Which is good.

Because I'm Billy Boston. And when everyone is lame and sleeping, or sexy and sleeping in one case, that's when I do the real work. That's when it's really playtime. I reach for my phone.

Me: *Yo, Murph. You still know that guy with a horse?*

Murphy: *Yeah, he owes me a favor. What do you got in mind, motherfucker?*

Me: *Don your fanciest suit and hat. We're putting on the Boston derby in the Common tonight.*

I don't get a text back. Because Murph is already busy gathering horses from his horse guy. He's single too, so he still remembers what's supposed to happen after the sun goes down. How to live life to the fullest.

I'm going to turn this day into a night to remember —one that is so much fun I won't be able to remember most of it tomorrow.

And before I do that, I shall be partaking in a gentleman's shower. I will take out all of my frustrations on my rod by imagining there *isn't* a wall between me and the beautiful nurse next door. That she really did turn to put her hands against the wall, spreading her legs and pushing her luscious apple-bottom ass out, teasing and offering herself to me at the same time. And that I am the one ripping that little silk dress off her, giving her sweet, sweet drain a plunging she'll never forget.

donna

WHAT LARS BEQUEATHED

Five minutes until I arrive at the farmhouse, according to my GPS. More like four minutes until I get to the stretch where the GPS will lose its shit and I'll probably lose cell phone service and then some guy in a mask will walk out to the middle of the deserted road, force me to stop my car, and stab me to death.

Oooh—a pumpkin patch!

I should stop by there on my way home if I don't get murdered.

For the forty-odd minutes I've been driving so far, I've been thinking of all the reasons why I should just try to sell the Olander farmhouse. The six acres of land is worth more than the eighty-year-old house, so it doesn't really make sense to fix it up before selling it anyway. And it certainly doesn't make sense for me to live on a huge remote property all by myself. Especially when I'd have to drive forty-five minutes to and from work.

Except Middleborough is so nice and the historic downtown is so quaint and I have such a clear vision of what the house could be.

And even if I only came out here two days a week when I have time off, it would be worth it to keep it.

And I could never afford this kind of secluded property on a nurse's salary, no matter how long I save for. This is an incredible gift.

That property meant a lot to Lars, and it means a lot to me that he wanted me to have it.

Except now I have to pay rent on my apartment *and* the property taxes on this place because he left all of his money to charities.

And there's something about that house that's creepy as fuck.

But I refuse to be scared of anything.

I can do this.

I should really be sleeping on my day off, but I think I can get tons of cleaning done this time, then be out of there an hour before the sun starts to go down.

I turn onto the tree-lined road that leads to the lane that leads to the house that Lars built. The trees form a lovely canopy over the two-lane road, and it's really very peaceful. As long as there aren't any mask-wearing, axe-wielding murderers around.

But just in case, I call my friend Chelsea. It rings

once. Twice. "Come on—pick up, pick up, pick up." She should be at her desk at the office.

She answers before the fourth ring. "Why aren't you asleep right now?"

"Oh, thank God."

"What's wrong?"

"Nothing. I'm definitely not scared. Just don't hang up."

"Oh no. Are you goin' to that Bulgarian lady for a bikini wax again?"

That makes me laugh. "No. Never again. I'm going to the house in Middleborough."

"Ohhhhh. You mean *your* house? The one Lars left you in his will?" Chelsea is the coordinator for the home health-care agency I work for, so she knows all about Lars. She's actually the one who assigned me to him a year and a half ago.

"Sort of. He had his lawyer create a trust for me so it wouldn't have to go through probate."

"Nice. I thought you said you ran outta there last time."

"Yeah, I think I just got there too late in the day. When the weather was bad. And it's just a drafty old house that creaks and moans, you know? For normal old-house reasons. But I got spooked. And the weather's nice today, so I figured I'd give it another shot." I slow down to turn onto the lane that leads to the property. I can't help but sigh. It's so pretty. Just a symphony of fall colors and the morning light hitting the water of the pond—my very own pond! "Oh my God, Chels, I can't wait for you to see this place. The cranberry bog. It's so beautiful. I mean, it's surreal. But it's really beautiful."

"That reminds me, I gotta buy cranberry juice. I feel a UTI comin' on."

"Save your money—I can make you some!" I park my car in the driveway in front of the house. There's a detached garage that I haven't even looked inside yet. Popping in my earbuds, I open the car door, marveling at how still and quiet it is. I instantly feel ridiculous about being so scared the last time I was here. It's so peaceful and wonderful. "You still there?"

"Yeah. I'm mainlinin' coffee and replyin' to five thousand emails. Keep talkin'. You at the house? Shoot me a picture."

I do. I take a few steps back to get the entire two-story Colonial revival house in frame, with its wrap-around porch and the shutters and the brick chimneys that extend from the ground past the roof on both sides of the house. "You can tell it was wonderful when it was first built in the late 1940s," I tell her before texting the picture to her.

She's quiet for way too long and then says, "Joel knows a really good but somewhat shady Realtor who could sell a pile of dirt to a prince. I'll grab you his contact info."

"I mean, it needs some work—obviously it hasn't been lived in for decades. Lars said he hired people to update things back in the early seventies so he could rent the place out, but they never finished the job. Like, everyone he hired would just stop working there after about a week. 'Damn hippies,' he said. 'No work ethic.' So he took it as a sign that he should be more picky about who lives here. And I guess I'm the only one he picked. But it could be so perfect. Right? It has good bones. If you saw this on *Fixer Upper* you would be like, *I cannot wait to see what Chip and Joanna do with that place.*"

"Okay, honey, okay. What's that shadow in the upstairs window?!"

"What?!" My heart is suddenly in my throat as I look up at the upstairs windows.

"Just kiddin'. I'm fuckin' with you."

I exhale loudly, my pulse still racing. "That is really not cool."

I scan the entire area, turning on my heels because I have the strangest feeling I'm being watched.

A crow caws overhead, and I almost scream, then laugh at myself for being so jumpy.

Okay, there's a little bit of mist rolling in, so that changes the atmosphere a little bit, but it's still sunny. I face death on a regular basis at work. What do I have to be afraid of?

I walk up the steps to the porch and fumble with my keys.

"Why didn't Lars sell the farmhouse a long time ago if he was living in a townhouse in Charlestown? Also why didn't he leave you the townhouse in Charlestown?"

"Because he was renting it." Opening the front door, I peer inside before entering. The air seems... stale? Heavy? Sad? Obviously that's just my imagination. Air can't be sad. It just needs to circulate. I step inside the vestibule, leaving the door open—to air the place out. "He, uh, Lars had the farmhouse built for his wife when they got married back in the late 1940s."

I open the interior door to the front hall. I definitely don't remember shutting this door on my way out last time, but of course it would close on its own if there are drafts. See? Logic. There's a logical explanation for everything.

"It's really sad, actually," I continue as I look up the staircase in the middle of the center hall. The last time I was up there in the master bedroom I thought I heard someone crying and whispering, and that was when I bolted out of here. But it was probably just a breeze.

"Lars and his wife were young and in love, and he bought the property with a cranberry bog thinking they'd harvest cranberries, have a working farm, and raise a family here. He said his wife loved it so much and it was the happiest he'd ever seen her." The hard-

47

wood floor creaks with every step I take. I go into the dining room to open the windows. "But then his wife got pneumonia and died after living here for only a matter of months. Lars was too sad to live here without her, and he could never bring himself to sell the place." I struggle with the window, which seems to be painted shut. "He hired people to maintain and harvest the cranberry bog, but nobody's been living in the house and he hadn't been back here in decades."

The two front doors slam shut in quick succession, and I spin around, my heart racing even faster than it did when I heard the crow. "Holy shit!"

"What happened?!"

But of course the doors slammed shut. I didn't prop them open. I hesitantly make my way back to the front hall. Nothing to see here, except for a closed door. Shaking my head, I cross the hall to the living room to try opening some windows in there.

"Nothing. Just a light breeze. It was nothing."

"*Ohhh-kaaayyyy*. So did Lars ever remarry?" Chelsea asks.

"No. Never met anyone he cared about as much as her."

"Until he met *yoooouuuu*," she says in a hushed voice.

"He cared about me like a granddaughter, Chelsea." I don't tell her that when he told me he wanted the property to pass to me he mentioned it

48

was situated near Assawompset Pond, so it made sense for me to live there. I try not to read into that. Ever. "He was a sweet, lonely old man with no family, and I liked him."

These living room windows are easier to open. Heavy and a bit sticky, but I can lift them open. I run my fingertips along the molding around the big window. It's dusty, but everything here seems solid. It just needs to be lived in. And brought into this century.

I notice that I have goose bumps on my forearms and that reminds me to turn up the heat. As I pass through the room to adjust the thermostat, I remember there is no thermostat. Because this house was built in the late 1940s. I brought a space heater with me last time. I think I left it upstairs in the bedroom.

"It is sweet that he was your buddy," Chelsea says. "Oh shit, I almost forgot! Joel finally has a new guy working in his office who's recently divorced and kinda cute and probably not a creep. You gotta come to dinner with us—we'll do a double date."

"I don't date, Chels, you know that."

"Still?"

I freeze when I hear the floor creak upstairs.

I think.

Did I? It could have been the floor creaking beneath my feet, and it just sounded like it came from upstairs. Or there's probably mice and who knows what other kinds of critters living in the attic. They're probably super cute, like Disney cartoon animals, who are more scared of me than I am of them. We could peacefully coexist, and they'll sing to me while helping me clean and get me dressed for a Halloween ball.

"Babe, it's been, like, two years since Trevor..." She doesn't finish that sentence because the sentence would end with *dumped you and moved to Florida after you left Philly to go to the same college as him.* Or something along those lines.

"It has nothing to do with Trevor," I say with a tremor in my voice. "I just don't have time to date."

"Ohhhh, I see why you like that house. It reminds you of your neglected, cobwebby vulva."

"Actually, my vulva is very well tended to, thank you so much."

"By what?"

"By my no-strings guy." With a deep, shaky breath, I gather my courage and head for the stairs.

"What no-strings guy?"

"My neighbor. I told you. We've had this thing for well over a year now."

"Wait, not the neighbor you were always complaining about when you first moved to that apartment? The one who'd blast Chumbawamba late at night?"

"Yeah. That one. But he's changed a lot. Now he uses headphones to listen to that song."

"Well, I don't like you being out there by yourself, and I can't leave work. I'd send Joel over, but he's at work too. Why don't you call your friendly neighbor to come help you, Donna? He sounds like the kind of guy who doesn't have regular office hours. Someone who can help you get back up again when you get knocked down..."

That makes me laugh again. "Accurate. But that would be breaking the no-strings rule. We have a pact about this kind of thing. It's just sex. We don't get involved in each other's personal lives. And I don't need help. It's just a house. I'm just going to do some cleaning. I can handle it all by myself. You get back to work. I'm fine, really. Don't worry about me."

"You text me when you leave and when you get home, and you call me if you need to talk again, okay? I've got an admin mess or five to clean up over here. Love ya."

"Love you—bye."

I feel better now. The very thought of calling Billy for anything other than a sex or party emergency is hilarious. Although I can't get over the fact that he actually fixed my dishwasher last night. And covered me with a blanket. That was pretty sweet. But I know he went out after that, so it's not like it meant anything to him. And that's fine. That's the deal. He gets it.

I remove the earbuds from my ears and drop them

into my shoulder bag. Now the house seems excruciat-ingly quiet. Expectant. Almost like it's anxiously listening for a response from me...

Which is also hilarious because houses don't have ears.

Ignoring the flutter of anxiety in my chest, I take one step up the staircase and wait. For what, I don't even know, but nothing happens. Nothing creaks. No hellmouth appears, swallowing me up and trapping me in the basement. Two more steps up and I stop in my tracks because I hear something that sounds an awful lot like an exasperated sigh. But it's probably steam seeping out of a pipe.

This is beyond ridiculous.

But I go out to my car to arm myself with a crow-bar, just in case.

"Nut up, Fischer," I say to myself as I ascend the stairs again, pride and curiosity winning the battle against apprehension. "I'm coming upstairs and I have a weapon!" I call out, hopefully just to some rodents and a leaky radiator.

Reaching the second-floor hallway, I am astutely aware of my elevated blood pressure and each and every hair that is standing up on the back of my neck. This terrible cocktail of excitement and trepidation feels very much like my reaction every time I've thought about the possibility of dating again ever since Trevor left. I am certainly not ready to face a serious relationship yet. But I am going to be the boss of this house, and it starts with returning to the master bedroom.

The bedroom door is closed. I don't remember closing it when I ran out last time, but again, why wouldn't it close on its own if this house is so drafty?

I have to pause when I'm a foot away from the door because I hear that sound again, more like a moan.

Definitely an old house sound.

I reach for the doorknob, but just as I do, the door pops open on its own.

And all I can hear is my own screams.

billy

I'm striding through the shiny waiting area of some fancy-schmancy offices in a downtown skyscraper that I would one day like to rappel off.

After I won the lottery, it was important to me not to just spend or waste all that money. I mean, don't get me wrong—I put it to good use for good times. But I wanted to do something productive with it as well. As part of my legacy, if you will. After consulting with my family, Declan and Nolan in particular, I founded a startup called the Locker Room.

It's an escape room meets a fantasy sports camp. To move on from one locked room to the next, you have to score the winning basket or catch the winning touchdown or punch the puck through on a fast break. It's the kind of place I would have spent all my time at when I was a kid, and it's been a huge success right out of the gate. So we're scaling rapidly and opening new locations all across New England. If all goes well, and there's no reason it wouldn't, we'll be all over the East Coast by the second quarter next year. National by the end of next year.

Is it exciting? Sure. Am I nervous? Nah. Do I like making a shit ton of money? It doesn't hurt. But I was happy before I was a millionaire, and I'm no more or less happy now.

I tip my hat to the receptionist and see myself into the boardroom. All of my executives are already seated. I remove my derby hat and drop it in front of me at the head of the long, impressive oak table. I'm still wearing the pastel pinstripe suit and suspenders I put on when I left my apartment last night. I never used to explain the *why*s and the *what*s and the *how*s of what I did and wore before I got rich. Now that I'm a boss I explain even less. It's fucking awesome. But if anyone wants to know about the Boston derby I organized last night with a couple of my friends and about a hundred friendly strangers, I would be happy to tell them.

"Good morning, everyone," I say as I take my seat.

"Good morning, Mr. O'Sullivan," my team replies.

I lean back in my executive chair, stretching out and stacking my boots on the table. The boots are clean—I'm not a filthy animal. "What's first up on the agenda today, ladies and gents?"

"We need to discuss the Make-A-Wish partnership," my chief financial officer says.

I lower my feet and lean forward, resting my forearms on the table instead. "Shoot."

"The foundation has the budget to pay travel and lodging fees as well as the going rate for the cost of the use of our facilities. But I was wondering if you—"

I cut him off with a wave of my hand. "No, we pay for everything. They just tell us where and when and whatever they need—it's on us."

"That's very generous and it's what I figured you'd say, Mr. O'Sullivan. Thank you."

"What else?" I look around the room. This meeting could have been an email, but I like the face-to-face aspect of it. "Whaddya got for me?"

"The promo event with Make-A-Wish..." says Grace, my chief marketing officer. Or my head of marketing. Or my VP of marketing. Whatever she is, she's great.

"What about it? What can I do to make it awesome?"

"Will you be attending?"

"Of course."

"Fantastic," she says, holding up her iPad. "Will you be...bringing someone? A plus-one?"

I immediately think of Donna. Which is silly. Because Donna and I aren't dating. But it just seems like the kind of event she'd enjoy if she actually had the night off.

But Grace is eyeing me, like she's expecting me to bring someone in particular. I shift around in my seat. "Do you...think I should bring someone?"

She clears her throat, looking just as uncomfortable as I currently feel. "It's entirely up to you, sir. It's just...I need to know the...um, *type* of person you're bringing so I can properly plan for..."

"Oh. Oooooohhhh. I hear ya. You're concerned about Murph."

Grace furtively glances around at her colleagues for support before saying, "Not concerned, exactly, no! Mr. Murphy brings a tremendous energy to any event he attends, but it can be—"

Once again, I hold up my hand, silencing an employee. I'm sure she's thinking of the last time I brought my boy Michael Murphy to a Locker Room event. He dressed as the mascot for our city's occasionally great football franchise—a tomcat. There were a bunch of other mascots for other football teams at the event because we were hoping to expand beyond New England posthaste. But pictures turned up online of a big, furry, angry, man-sized cat wrestling with various other man-sized animals, and from certain angles it did look as though he humping them. So we collectively decided to take a step back until those images are but a distant seventh or eighth page Google search result. And it was a good thing too—made more sense to get a foothold in New England before dominating the nation and then the world anyway.

Still, the last time I saw Murph, he was riding the winning horse, Jeepers Creepers, across the finish line at our impromptu midnight derby and then off into the sunrise, so...Grace is not wrong to have concerns. "I will not be bringing Murphy as my plus-one, Grace. I will be attending said event with a date. An unnamed female woman date of the highest order."

"Wonderful!" she exclaims, typing something into her iPad. She seems very satisfied with my response, and the meeting continues without requiring my attention or input.

Myself, I am less than satisfied. I mean, I'd be happy to bring my ma, but it would be nice to have, like, one other option who's not Murph. The girls I've hooked up with in the past have lived in the land between 10:00 p.m. and 4:00 a.m. Part of my epic, drunken adventures. My love life, if one could even call it that, is like a vampire. It's a creature of the night, destroyed by sunlight.

I pull out my cell phone, thinking about finally downloading a dating app, but I find a text from Donna. A daytime text from Donna. What do ya know.

Red: *Hi. I have the day off. What are you doing right now?*

58

Me: *Hey. That depends. What would you like me to be doing right now?*
Red: *I need you to meet me at the following address ASAP.*

She sends an address in Middleborough, which is, like, a forty-five minute drive from here.

Me: *Should I bring anything?*
Red: *Just come as fast as you can. Be Mark Wahlberg from the movie Fear. I'm a virgin and my parents are out of town. I am inviting you to come to my house. I will probably be lying in bed, virginally, waiting for you. Know what I mean?*
Me: *Fuck that guy. Fuck all the Wahlbergs. I'm cooler than all of them.*
Red: *<face with rolling eyes emoji> Just please get over here and take my virginity ASAP okay?!*

I grab my jaunty hat and excuse myself from the unfinished meeting—another perk of being the boss. I do a quick change in my corner office. Various wardrobes are now kept in various locations, including the trunk of my car, mostly for Donna reasons. Because I never know who I'll need to be at a moment's notice.

Speaking of—I swipe a Sharpie pen from my desk. Gonna need that for later.

Within ten minutes of Donna's last text I'm in my

Volvo and on the road to Middleborough. Traffic thins out the farther I get from Boston. Buildings give way to clusters of trees. In no time my GPS tells me I've arrived, and boy, have I ever. This property is beautiful. The house is too. Well, the landscape is a little overgrown and the house is a little neglected. There's some peeling paint, and I can tell those windows and doors need to be replaced. But this place has character out the ass. It's a little rough around the edges, but it's bursting with potential.

Like me.

Just waiting for the right person to see that potential and take it to the next level.

I really do feel at home in the world wherever I roam, but I have the strongest feeling that I could live here someday. I mean, not now. This place isn't the party. It's a vacation from the party. The quiet trip to the bathroom where the music is muted and you splash water onto your face and look at yourself in the mirror to ground yourself.

That's this place—a place to ground yourself, so you can go back and face the party again.

When I get out of the car I see Donna watching me through a downstairs window as she paces back and forth. She looks anxious. Impatient. Hopefully she's just super horny like I am since we didn't get to finish what we started last night.

I take the Sharpie pen out of my pocket and turn

around so Donna can't see what I'm doing. I pull my shirt up so I can write on my stomach, using the car window as a mirror. When I yank my shirt back down and turn back to face her she looks confused. I wink at her. Her expression goes blank, and she acts like she hasn't just seen me. Like she's just an innocent, super-hot, buxom teenager padding about the house, unaware that a virile, ripped young man who's totally obsessed with her is about to break the door down and take her virginity. Or something.

I stalk up to the house in my super tight shirt and baggy jeans and bang on the door. "Let me in the house!"

Donna frowns at me through the window next to the front door. "What are you doing?! That's from the wrong part of the movie!"

"You didn't specify which part you wanted to play out!"

"I very specifically said in the text!"

"Well, it's been a long time since I've seen the movie!" I'm still yelling like I'm obsessed with Donna the virgin. It's not much of a stretch—the concept has me pretty worked up.

She rolls her eyes, and I can't tell if she's mad or amused by me. "Oh my God!"

"So do you want me to be all sweet now? Like how he was in the beginning?"

"No, this is hot! Keep going!"

"Damn right I'm gonna keep goin'!" I rip my shirt off over my head and reveal that I've written *Donna4Eva* on my abs in Sharpie. Her eyes go wide in a very satisfying way. "It's me, Mahk Wahlberg, let me in the house! And say hi to your mothah for me, okay?" I do a pretty decent Wahlberg, even though I'm a way better dancer than that guy is and I would be way more famous than him if I gave a shit about any of that crap.

"Leave me alone!" Donna cries out, impressively quivering.

"I can't. I'm obsessed with youse. I can't stop thinking about youse. Open the door!"

I hear her unlock the dead bolt. "Just don't break down the door," she wails over-dramatically, clearly wanting me to "break down the door."

I kick the door in. She gasps, one hand covering her mouth, the other hand dramatically clutching her ample bosom. She acts like a cornered animal, whimpers, turns, and runs up the stairs. I chase after her. I could overtake her, but I really enjoy watching her ass shift back and forth in those sweatpants as her legs pump their way up the steps.

I grab at her ass like I'm trying to stop her, but really I'm just grabbing at her glorious bottom. "You're mine, Donna! Mine!"

"Her name's Nicole!" she pants. "Yours is David!"

"Whatevah! That ass is mine, Nicole!"

She squeals, and just as she's about to burst through what I imagine is the bedroom door, she comes to a sudden stop. I stop in my tracks right behind her. I turn her around, thinking that she's making some interesting acting choices, when I recognize actual fear on her pretty face.

"What's wrong?" I ask, no longer in character.

She shakes her head and steps aside, genuinely trembling. "You go in first. Okay?"

"Yeah, of course," I say, a little confused. Is this a trap or something? Maybe her angry protective dad's in there waiting for me.

Donna's pressed up against my back, holding on to my bare shoulders.

I open the closed door, peering inside before stepping through the doorway. It is indeed a bedroom. Empty, so far as I can tell. Dusty and clearly not lived in for a long time, but it's comfortable. There's a four-poster bed and some tables and ornate lamps. A chandelier hanging from the center of the ceiling.

It doesn't *look* strange. But it feels strange. The air is oddly heavy and stale. No, not stale. Like all the sound has been sucked out of it. That surreal, heavy thickness is pierced by scratching from behind another door in the room. My attention snaps to it. Just a normal, brown wooden door.

"Is that door the closet?" I ask Donna, my voice is not echoing like it should in a mostly empty room like this. Instead, all sound kind of drops and thuds into the walls and hardwood floor. I turn and discover that she didn't follow me into the room. She's standing at the threshold, holding her hands tightly in front of her chest.

"I think so," she says meekly.

"Whose house is this?" I finally ask.

"*Mm-mmmine?*"

"Donna, what's wrong?"

She squeezes her eyes shut and shakes her head, hugging herself.

I hear that scratching sound again and look to the door again.

Fuck this.

I stalk toward that door like I have *Door4Eva* written on my abs. I'm not afraid. I *am* Fear. Mark Fear. Or David Fear, or whatever the fuck Wahlberg's name was in the movie.

I fling the door open. It's so creaky, it practically screams.

I just see darkness in there. Emptiness. It's somehow even creepier than seeing a monster.

And then there's a frantic burst of movement. I duck down just in time. Donna screams.

There's flapping. Feathers. Cooing. A mourning dove.

I run to the nearest window, open it, and then encourage the dove to fly out of it by blocking the door and waving my arms around. After a few false starts, the poor thing makes it out. I shut the window a bit too hard, adrenaline coursing through me.

The air doesn't feel thick anymore. Maybe because Donna and I are heaving so much of it into our lungs.

"How did it get in here? I couldn't open that window the last time I was here," she murmurs. She's talking to herself, not me. She looks so flustered and confused.

"Are you okay?"

"That's what the moaning and whispering sounds were," she says, still lost in thought.

"Yeah, it was just a—" My mouth snaps shut when Donna locks her wild green eyes with mine.

Suddenly they aren't crazed with fear, they're burning hot with desire. She jumps up on me, wrapping her arms around my shoulders and her legs around my waist. She makes high-pitched noises like a starving girl as she kisses me frantically, deeply. The momentum of everything she's doing to me pushes me back against the wall. I give those round, bountiful ass cheeks a firm squeeze. I did not have *creepy old bird-infested house* on my sex bingo card, but this is doing it for both of us.

I break the kiss even though she doesn't make it easy. "I don't remember Reese Witherspoon being this forward in the movie."

"Just go with it, David," she says in a voice that

probably wasn't meant to sound so husky and womanly, but I'm digging it.

"Yes, *and...*" I improvise, kissing her again and carrying her over to the bed. "I'm gonna take your sweet virginity so fucking beautifully you're gonna remember it forever, Nicole."

"Hard—take it hard!"

"I'm gonna take your sweet fuckin' v-card so fuckin' hard you're gonna feel my rock-hard cock pounding your hot, wet pussy for the rest of your life, you naughty girl."

We fall onto the mattress, but she's so full of energy she flips over on top of me. "I'm so nervous and scared but also so curious!" she says, all breathless, straddling me and caressing the words I scrawled across my abs just for her.

I reach for her top to remove it, but she bats my hands away and takes it off herself. Donna with her hair up in a ponytail, dressed in a flimsy old T-shirt is the present you've been asking for all year. It's wicked hot when the Christmas present aggressively unwraps itself. She stares down at me as she tosses that shirt away. Daylight floods the room through dusty windows, and it is so fucking magnificent to see her like this. It's usually nighttime, dimly lit when we're together. Her pale skin is dazzling. Flushed with pink, and even though it's warm to the touch, she has goose bumps all over.

She dips down and kisses me hungrily again. Her tits press against my chest, and we both work to unhook her bra. When we do she lets that bra drop. I break the kiss again to get a good look at her gorgeous naked torso when she sits upright. She's breathing so hard and rocking back and forth on my johnson. Bouncing and jiggling and so fucking hot I might pass out because all the blood in my body is rushing to the part of me that's dying to be inside her right now. "Jesus fuck, you are so beautiful, Donna."

"Nicole."

I reach for her, but she wrestles with me, pinning my arms down over my head as she lowers one breast to my mouth. I accept it hungrily. Sucking and swirling my tongue. I do feel like a teenager. I am so lost in lust for her I have no idea who I'm supposed to be—I just know that I have never wanted to fuck anyone so bad in my life.

"It feels so good, David!"

"You are so fuckin' hot, baby. I wanna kiss you all ovah."

"Yeah, I want that."

"You want that?" I flip her onto her back so fast and rough, she gasps. Then I nip at the flesh of her waist and lick all the way up and around those mounds of heaven, flicking at her hard pink nipples with my tongue. "You like that, little virgin, huh?"

"Yeah, don't stop."

"I ain't evah gonna stop, baby girl." I kiss my way down her belly and then yank her sweatpants down, pressing my lips against her warm, wet cotton panties. "Let me in the panties!" We both laugh but quickly get serious again when I lap up the elixir at the sweet, hot center of her. "You taste so good, Donna—Nicole —baby."

She whimpers and trembles, but in a totally different way from how she was trembling and whimpering a few minutes ago. "No one ever gets me this wet, Billy—I mean, David—only you."

"Huh? I thought you're a virgin." Fuck it, who cares who we are. "I'm gonna eat you out until you beg me to stop."

"Yes! Tell me what you're gonna do!"

"I'm gonna fuck your angel pussy with my tongue, and you're gonna scream my name and *oh God* so many times you'll think I'm God."

"Yeah! Do it!" Then she groans. "Wait. Shit. Wait, stop. I have to finish cleaning the house before the sun goes down."

"Huh? Your parents makin' you do chores while they're out of town?"

"What?" She wriggles around, freeing herself from her pants and panties. "Just take my virginity now— hurry up." She repositions herself so her head rests on a pillow, clasping her hands over her chest. "But take me however you want me."

"Yep, that also works." I pop up, pull a condom packet from my pocket, and then let my jeans and my Calvin Klein boxer briefs—that look ten times hotter on me than they ever did on Marky Mark—drop to the floor. Donna watches me roll the condom on, biting her swollen lower lip and then swallowing hard because her mouth is watering for my cock. "Your mouth is watering for my cock, isn't it?"

She nods.

"You ready for it?"

She nods, shyly.

"Get on your hands and knees and face the headboard."

She does.

I nearly choke on my tongue, staring at that beautiful naked ass.

On her hands and knees, she glances over her shoulder at me and bats her eyelashes all innocently.

I tease her entrance, and it's killing me.

"Hold on to the headboard. Hold on tight."

She does. When I see that she has a good grip on it, I ram into her. She cries out, but there's so much pleasure in that sound.

"Good?"

"Yeah. More."

I give her more. I give her everything I've got. Gripping her waist as hard as she's gripping the edge of the headboard. The posts beat against the wall with a staccato rhythm. The crystal beads of the chandelier above us rattle and clink against each other, but it's not to the same tempo as my thrusts. I'm aware of that thing that's pulsing overhead like there's an earthquake, but the house could split in two and it wouldn't stop me from fucking this woman.

Her head's swaying like she's in ecstasy, but when I grab her ponytail and arch her neck back, that's when she shudders and screams my name and then spasms around my cock. *My* name. Billy. I work so hard to keep from coming until after the tornado of an orgasm has ripped through her. I keep going and going and going, sweat dripping into my eyes, until she goes limp for a few seconds.

Then she braces herself again and tells me, her voice hoarse and just above a whisper, that she wants to come again, with me. I give her ass a smack and pull out of her, moving fast, because *out* is the opposite direction from where I want to be when it comes to her. But we've had sex so many times I know she likes to ride me, so I get onto my back and let her climb on top of me. Watching her grip the base of my erection. Watching her lower herself down onto it. Watching her play with her tits as she rocks her hips back and forth and then round and round, slow at first. My eyelids are so heavy and my vision is so blurry, but I force myself to see as much as I can.

Resting my hands on her thighs, I have to

squeeze my eyes shut for a minute because every-thing about this is so fucking good I'm torn—completely torn between the desire to make this last forever and the need to explode and disappear into this wild, furious madness I feel for her today. I don't know what's gotten into her, but it's in me too. I feel her pressing down on my chest. Bearing down on me. Arching her back, her neck. She's ramping things up.

I spank her ass, real quick, and the surprise sends an intense shudder through her. She clamps around my cock, and there she goes again. With a gentle massage of my chest, she wordlessly signals to me that I can surrender to the storm I've been quelling.

I do.

With a howl, I let it tear through me. I'm aware of her leaning back as I empty myself, hot and heavy, inside of her, into the condom, so much that it spills out. I'm aware that the bedposts are still banging against the wall, the chandelier is still rattling. But I can't hear anything except the muted echo of my roar, like I'm driving through a tunnel in slow motion. This orgasm seems to last forever.

It seamlessly leads me into a deep sleep, I guess. I have a bizarre, vivid dream about the house we're currently in. A woman lives here in the dream. But Donna and I also live here. And not as roommates. As something more. Way more. But it's not scary in the dream. Neither is the house. We're not trapped in it. We're protected by it.

"It was waiting for you," the woman says. Her voice echoes in a strange way, the opposite of the thudding in this room.

"For us?" I ask. Donna is next to me, but I can't see her. Only feel her.

The woman nods and looks past me. I look over my shoulder, but everything slows down. I hear the patter of feet behind. Small feet. And giggles. Kid giggles. I can't turn enough to see them. Everything is too slow, and then darkness.

When I wake up, Donna's lying on top of me. We're both slick with sweat. The room is still filled with soft golden daylight. The chandelier is so still I might have imagined it shaking before.

Now there's a gentle, quiet stillness that's so peaceful it's kind of weird.

For a few seconds, I panic because it feels like something's holding me down. Not Donna's body, but some force is keeping me on this bed. I try to move my fingers, but I can't.

Am I still dreaming?

Donna twitches and then inhales, slowly rolling off me.

I'm able to breathe again. I'm able to move my fingers. "Seriously, what is this place?" I mumble when I finally remember how to talk.

Donna clears her throat. "I inherited it. I mean, it was left to me. By a patient of mine who passed away a few months ago."

"So you actually own this house?"

"Yup."

"Oh. Does that mean you're gonna move here?" As much as I felt some kind of connection to this place when I drove up, I hate the thought of Donna not being my neighbor anymore.

She sighs. "I don't know. Not any time soon." She tries to sit up but plops back down. "So that was good, huh?"

"Yeah." I chuckle. "Pretty good. Bathroom?"

Donna points to an open door next to the closet. I kiss her on the forehead and climb off the bed to clean myself up. The door to the en suite bathroom is already open. It's huge and in better shape than it has any right to be. I'm starting to see the house a little differently now that I know it's hers. It's somewhere between a playground, a project, and a threat.

"So. Big night last night?" Donna asks from the other room.

"Always." I pop my head out of the bathroom and give her an eyebrow waggle.

She walks over to me, wearing only her T-shirt and panties. Her hair's so chaotic, and she literally can't walk straight.

I'm very proud.

"Did you have a hot date?" She leans against the door frame, sounding pretty casual, as if it's normal for us to be chatting about this kind of thing, which it isn't—but there's something strange in her voice.

"Nah, not like that. You know I don't date."

"Oh yeah, of course, I was joking." Great actress, terrible liar.

"Although I do need a date pretty soon. I mean, first there's my granny's birthday party and then there's a PR thing for work."

"Oh yeah?" She doesn't ask what work is for me, but I'm pretty sure she still has no idea.

"Yeah. I realized I don't know how normal people do it. How do you just ask a girl to a thing like that? Like, when you're both sober? Do *you* know how to date?"

Donna laughs. A beautiful, joyful sound. "Of course I know how. For me *not dating* is a choice."

"I thought it was for me too, but now I'm seeing it's my only option at the moment." *Why don't you come with me?* is on the tip of my tongue. I almost say it. After all, I'm the guy who says whatever's on his mind.

But I don't.

Because if I even ask her out as a joke she could end this.

I turn on the faucet. Nothing happens at first, which shouldn't surprise me. Water to the house might not even be on. Then the pipes behind the wall start to rattle. Not *I'm trying to get going after some years* kind of rattle but an *I'm angry you're trying to do this* rattle. There's a whine. No, a moan. That's the only way I can describe it. A moan coming from behind the wall.

"Whoa," I mutter. "Have you used the water here before?"

Donna shakes her head. "Not up here."

All of sudden, liquid starts pouring from the faucet.

But it's not clear. I don't even think it's water.

It's a deep, purplish red. Holy shit.

It's blood.

"What the hell!?" I yell.

Donna screams and covers her mouth.

I don't know why, maybe to confirm what I'm seeing, I turn on the faucet to the bathtub. Blood pours out of it as well, pooling at the bottom of the white porcelain like it's a scene out of *Psycho*.

"Billy..." Donna moans, terror gripping her.

I grab her hand, ready to pull her out of there. "Donna, let's... Hang on." I sniff the air. "Wait a minute," I murmur. I get in close to the blood that's still pouring out of the tap and sniff again. Now I'm sure.

I let go of Donna's hand and cup a handful of the "blood" to drink it down.

"Billy! What are you doing!" Donna screams.

I smile and smack my lips, calmly turning off both faucets.

"Are you a vampire or something?" she asks earnestly. Not like our role-play but like she's sure that I am and she's just crossing her t's and dotting her i's before I suck her tits like a creature of the night.

"Donna, is there a cranberry bog around here?"

"Yeah it... Wait. Cranberry juice?"

I nod.

"How on earth would cranberries get into the plumbing system?"

I shrug. "Weird shit happens with old houses, Fischer."

Donna groans. "No kidding. There's a lot of weird shit going on here. This place has so much potential, but it needs so much work. And I don't have the time. Or the money. I mean, I have savings, but I'd have to get a loan."

I have time and money is what I want to tell her. That gives me an idea. "Let me help you fix this place up."

"I can't ask you to do that."

"You're not askin', I'm offerin'. And this is a better place to role-play than your apartment. We can be as loud as we want out here."

"Yeah, no one can hear you scream," she says wryly, folding her arms in front of herself.

"But also, no one can hear me *make* you scream," I say suggestively. I place my hand over her folded arms. "I *vant* to fix up your house," I say in my best sexy vampire accent.

She laughs but doesn't look convinced. "It's a very sweet offer, Billy. But it's way too much to take on."

A house is nothing. I'd take on the world for you. It's a silly thought. I don't know where it comes from, and I don't voice it. Instead I say, "How's about we make a deal. You teach me how to date, and I help you with your house. You fix me up; I fix this place up."

She studies my face, and I watch her consider this proposal from all angles. I love watching her think. "Okay," she finally says. "Deal."

"Deal." I offer my hand, and we shake on it.

This is good. Everyone wins. Donna gets her house fixed; I get tips on modern, normal-person dating.

And if I get to spend more time with Donna, that doesn't seem so bad.

If Donna maybe gets a little bit jealous thinking about the other women she's teaching me to be with?

That's not the worst thing in the world either.

donna

NIGHT OF THE LIVING DATE

I spritz a little more perfume behind my ears and toss the bottle back into my handbag. After doing a twelve-hour shift at Mrs. Amato's house, I changed into a simple black dress and high-heeled boots in her powder room. I didn't want to look *too* good tonight, since it's not really a date, but then Mrs. Amato asked me whose funeral I was going to at this hour, and I'm thinking I may have veered a little too far in the not-sexy direction. So at least I'll smell hot.

Billy wanted to pick me up at work or at least drive me to the restaurant from the apartment, but I insisted on meeting him there. Lines are already being blurred, what with him helping to fix up my house and me helping to fix him up in the dating department, and then there was the dream I had about us back at the house...of us living there together and having kids... I think it's important for us to remember that we're just two people who live next door to each other who screw each other while pretending to be other people.

I've never been to Monarch before, but I've heard of it. Rooftop northern Italian fine dining on top of a fancy hotel in Back Bay. I heard they book reservations months in advance, but Billy said he knows a guy and managed to get us a table within forty-eight hours. Normally I don't waste money on valet parking —*normally* I take the T—but Billy insisted he'd cover the parking fee, and well, it's raining. When I pull up to the hotel, I see a gorgeous man in a beautiful suit shooting the shit with a few uniformed valets.

To my surprise, when said gorgeous, suited man turns and sees me in my Honda, I realize it's Billy. Based on how he's usually dressed around the apartment, it wouldn't have surprised me if I found out he worked as a valet here. The way he looks tonight, I would believe it if he told me he owned the place. He straightens his tie and combs his fingers through his wavy brown hair. Looks like he got a haircut. Looks good.

Goddamn it, he looks really good.

People are going to think I'm his grieving cousin.

He saunters around the front of my car and opens the door for me. "Greetings," he says, holding out his hand. "Lovely to see you, Donna."

I'm inwardly giggling, but outwardly I just nod at

him as I take his hand, trying not to think about all the incredible things that hand has done to my body in the past year or so, and say, "Sup?"

As he pulls me up and out of the driver seat, he leans in to whisper into my ear, "You *are* Donna tonight, right?"

Goddamn it, he smells really good too. Like whiskey and pumpkin spice and a mysterious, fancy cabin in the woods. "Yeah," I tell him, "I am. And you're Billy Boston."

A megawatt smile lights up his handsome face. "Fuck yeah, I am." He waves one of the valet parkers over. "Joey! You take extra special care of this Honda, you hear me?" He presses a twenty-dollar bill into Joey's palm.

"You got it, Billy."

Billy winks at me and places his hand on the small of my back as he leads me through the entrance to the lobby. "You look beautiful, Donna," he says into my ear again. "And you smell amazing."

His breath is warm and minty, and if my stomach dips and my knees wobble the tiniest bit, I'm sure it's because I'm hungry and I'm not used to wearing high heels anymore. "Thank you. My patient said I look like I'm going to a funeral."

"You look like someone any guy would wanna bury his stick in is what I say," he mutters.

And perhaps I shouldn't find that flattering as we

stroll across this marble lobby floor, but I do. "Why, thank you. You look very handsome."

He presses the elevator call button and smooths down the front of his suit jacket. "Thanks. How'm I doin' so far?"

Oh. So the whole compliment thing was all part of Date School. Good for him.

"So far you get an A, young man."

He rubs his chin with his thumb. "What's a guy gotta do to get an A-plus, huh, Miss Fischer?"

Just keep doing what you're doing is what I'm thinking. But I roll my eyes and smirk. "Extra credit is considered on a case-by-case basis."

The elevator dings and the doors slide open. Billy waits until the group of people disembark and walk past us before saying, "Well, in this case, I hope you'll consider me a very eager student." He holds his arm out, ushering me into the elevator car. "Who's willin' to break the rules to please his favorite teacher, if you know what I mean."

Do I ever.

When I step inside the elevator, I press my back up against the side wall and clutch my handbag to my chest, like I'm afraid he's going to steal it along with the rapidly beating heart that's hiding behind it. Billy jabs at the button for the top floor and languidly leans against the opposite wall, resting his hands on the brass railing behind him, his groin ever so casually thrust in my direction. A muffled, instrumental version of "Werewolves of London" is being piped through the speakers overhead. I watch as his gaze travels up the front of me, from the tips of my leather boots, lingering at my bare knees and lower thighs, up to my hips, and my scarlet-stained mouth.

Aside from his eyes, he is perfectly still. And that's when I realize Billy Boston is always moving. Alive in a way that few people are, especially in my world. Always talking. But right now he's holding himself back, and it's even more electrifying. Right now he's quiet and he's saying more than I can bear to understand.

If the air felt thick with something like sorrow at the farmhouse, the air in this elevator is thick with all the sexual tension between us. I don't even know how there could be so much tension between two people who've had sex as many times as we have. But it's there.

Before Billy's slow, hard stare meets mine, I drop my handbag to the floor and we both take two steps forward, meeting in a frantic kiss. My hands are cradling his face and his hands are all over my ass, and I want him to bury his stick six feet deep inside of me right here, right now.

"You are so fucking hot," he exhales.

"You look so fucking good in a suit."

"I look so fucking good in *you* too."

I am so confused by whether or not we're doing a scene right now because that's the kind of line he uses when we're role-playing. I can only respond by laughing. He kisses my neck.

"You think that's funny, Miss Fischer? I get an A-plus for that line?"

Ahh. He's playing hot for teacher. Not real. Got it. "Oh, you'll get what's coming to you in detention."

The elevator dings, and we bump foreheads as we bend down to pick up my handbag at the same time.

Now we're both laughing and swearing and wiping our mouths as we step off the elevator. "Do I have lipstick all over my face?" I ask him.

"Naw, you still look perfect," he says. "How about me?"

"Still handsome."

I silently praise my drugstore-brand lipstick for its staying power as he takes my hand.

"Is it okay for me to hold a girl's hand like this on a first date?"

"Yeah, I think it's nice."

"Cool."

I bump into him when I head toward the entrance to the restaurant and the crowd of well-dressed people waiting to be seated, just as he veers to the left. "We're goin' this way."

"Oh. I thought we were going to Monarch."

"We are. We're goin' in the special way."

And by that he means the service entrance.

He leads me down the hall and around the corner. There's a door with a keypad lock. He punches in a code and the door pops open. "Right this way, milady." We're in a back hall that leads to a very busy kitchen.

"Hey, Lorenzo!" Billy calls out to a middle-aged man in a jacket and tie, above the din of back-room chaos. "How are ya?"

"Hey, Billy! Where ya been?"

"I can't tell ya, but your ma says hi. Hey-oh! Here you go, my man." He presses a twenty-dollar bill into this guy's hand too, like it's no big deal.

Swagger.

Billy Boston has swagger as he struts through this busy commercial kitchen like he's John Travolta walking into a nightclub.

As we pass by the dishwasher stations, Billy punches a young man in the arm. "Gino! Lookin' fit, my man."

"Hey, Billy. I been takin' that protein powder I got from youse—that stuff is amazing."

"'Course it is. Lemme know when you need more."

Oh God, is Billy one of those nutritional-supplement affiliates? I would not be surprised if this is all some elaborate scheme to get me to buy a year's supply of creatine from him.

A very tall, dark-haired young man gives me the once-over when we walk past the salad prep station.

Billy squeezes my hand tight and gets right up in his face without missing a step. "Fuck you, Enzo. Don't you even look at my girl."

Enzo just looks away, no talking back. I have to say I'm a little turned on by IRL badass Billy.

Finally we're out of the kitchen and into the sophisticated, dimly lit, expansive restaurant, zigzagging through servers and tables.

Ahead of us, a distinguished elderly man in a dark suit is instructing a group of servers while pointing to different tables. He does a double take when he sees Billy approaching and immediately walks over to greet him, arms extended.

"Saverio!" Billy calls out to the man, who I'm assuming is the maître d'. "What's up, big guy?"

"Signore O'Sullivan! So nice to see you. Why we no see you in so long, huh? Did you call ahead? Nobody tell me."

"Naw, I thought I'd take my chances on a table for two." Billy scans the room and spots one free table in the back corner as he surreptitiously presses a hundo into Saverio's palm.

"But of course, yes, I have a very special table for you and the lady, of course!"

"This beautiful lady is Donna," Billy tells him with a flourish.

"*Buonasera, bella signora,*" Saverio says to me, holding out his hand.

"*Buonasera, signore.*" I hold out my hand, and he kisses it.

"*Buonasera.* Right this way, right this way." He snaps his fingers at a couple of servers, signaling to them as he leads us toward the table in the back. Before we reach it, candles on the table have been lit, water has been poured, and a young gentleman is waiting to hand us menus. Saverio pulls the table out himself to allow us a little more room to slide into the curved plush velvet booth, just as two other servers remove the chairs on the other side.

It's like they're moving heaven and earth for this guy.

Like, seriously, who is he?

"Thank you so much, Saverio," Billy says. "I owe ya."

"It is my pleasure, Signore O'Sullivan. If there is anything you need, you ask me."

And suddenly it's just me and *Signore O'Sullivan* at this corner table, under an ornate hanging lamp, flanked by potted tropical plants. Across from us is a window with sweeping views of Back Bay. I don't know that I'll ever catch my breath enough to actually eat, but Billy seems completely unfazed.

"Nice place, right?" he says, pushing his menu aside. "I always order the special."

"Come here a lot, do you?"

"I came here a lot a couple years ago, but I try to spread my money around, y'know?"

I cover my face, grinning and shaking my head. "Ahhh, you certainly do."

"What? I like good food. This place serves good food."

"No, I mean. The whole..." I wave my hand around and imitate him slapping money into guys' hands. "Hey, Matteo, whaddya say!"

He honestly does not seem to know what I'm talking about. "There's no one by the name of Matteo who works here."

"No, I mean—it's just a practice date. You can take it down, like, seven notches. You don't have to put on a big show."

"What big show?" He seems genuinely confused. "You mean in the elevator?"

"Nope. Never mind." I guess this is just how Billy rolls. Either that or he's a 1950s mob boss.

So, in the spirit of being a good date and showing him how it's done—I roll with that. I let him order for me—something I've never let a guy do before, not even Trevor—and to my great relief, everything he orders for us is just great. From the appetizers and tonight's special to the Chianti and dessert. If this is all an act, then he is an amazing actor.

If this is who he is when he's not pretending to be

someone else for my benefit, well...I think I like who he is.

The way he's leaning back with his arms spread out in the booth, manspreading under the table. The way his knee keeps touching mine every so often and he just smiles and winks in acknowledgment. I don't know. Any other guy and I'd probably find it obnoxious, but on Billy it's just...right.

I polish off my second glass of Chianti, since he assured me he'd have someone drive us home in my car. I'm feeling all warm and nice and beautiful and attended to. And then I remember I'm supposed to be teaching this guy how to behave on a first date. That's why we're here. In all honesty, in my opinion, most guys could learn a thing or two from him. But as I watch him laugh and chat with the diners who've stopped by our table to pay their respects to him or something, I do have some advice for him.

When the couple finally leaves and Billy asks me if I'd like more wine, I shake my head, lean into him a little, and say, "You know, Sir William..."

"Oh, I'm being knighted now?"

"Yes, Sir William. As your tutor, I do have an observation to make, if I may."

"By all means. Proceed."

"This is all great and kind of thrilling and very impressive." I swirl my hands around. "But one thing a lady would probably appreciate is to hear you get real, you know? Open up a little."

"Yeah?"

"I mean, if I were anyone other than me and this were an actual date, I'd really like to know what makes you tick. What's important to you?"

Billy's body language changes. He gets all serious, like he's really thinking about what to say. And just that, even, is so perfect. "Like, in general?" he asks.

"Just say whatever's on your mind. Tell me something important, big or small. Tell me something true about you."

He picks up his tumbler of whiskey on the rocks and clears his throat. "Well, Donna, I happen to have a lot of thoughts and feelings about life in general. I believe that I am doing things right and most people are missing out on the potential of what their lives could be. I believe life is for livin'. Y'know? I mean, *you* get it, right?"

"I do—I really do." He could have said he believes farts are messages from aliens and I would have agreed with him because I want to hear where this is going. I slow-blink at him, like a cat. A horny, tipsy cat who wants to curl up in his lap. But I don't. I place my elbow on the table and rest my chin on my fist and listen to him.

"Yeah, like, you're an old-people nurse, right?"

I chuckle at that. "I am a registered nurse specializing in geriatric care, yes."

"Yeah, so you probably know a lot of old people, and I bet none of them have ever said to you as they lay there on their deathbeds, 'Dammit, Donna, I just wish I'd lived a little less and tried fewer things and had less fun.' Right?"

"Absolutely correct."

"Now, I'm not talkin' about hittin' the clubs or any of that bullshit—sorry, is it okay for me to swear on a date?"

"I mean, it depends on who your fucking date is and whether or not you're swearing at her or around her, but in this case I will allow that shit."

He laughs. "Fuckin' A, Fischer. Fuckin' A." The skin around his eyes crinkles and his brown eyes sparkle when he smiles and laughs, all easygoing, and it's just so...appealing.

We just smile at each other for a few seconds, and I find myself leaning toward him even more and biting my lower lip as I stare at his mouth. That filthy, talented mouth, and then I remember that this isn't a real date—I'm here to teach him how to date someone else.

Clearing my throat, I straighten up and say, "In general, though, in the spirit of your edification, Sir William, I'd say people are expected to be on their best behavior for the first date. First through third date, even. And most would say that you should wait until you get a sense of whether or not your date would be offended by something before saying it. But honestly, I would rather know who a person is up front instead of finding out years into the relationship after I've moved to another state to go to college with him..." I smack my lips, realizing that I was about to reveal way more about my own personal history than necessary.

Billy's brow furrows. "Go on..."

"Nope! *You* go on. Tell me more of what you'd tell a date about your thoughts and feelings about life."

He studies me for an odd moment and then launches back into it. "Yeah, y'know. I just think life should be an adventure. I think people forget that. It's like, we know it instinctively as kids, right? We're born with that hunger. It's just like an innate intense curiosity about what this world we were born into is like.

"Learning is an adventure. That's the kind of fun I'm talking about. Learning what life can be. Learning who you are. Learning what your friends are made of. But most people, as soon as they start taking on responsibilities, it's like they think that means they aren't allowed to have fun anymore. A lot of people assume that just 'cause I like to have fun that means I'm irresponsible." He shrugs. "If drivin' a Volvo and payin' all your bills on time and makin' sure all your loved ones are taken care of doesn't count as bein' responsible, well, then I guess I'm not.

"But nobody ever got hurt on a night out with me. Yeah sure, a lot of crazy shit happens when you're open to it. Yeah, there's been hours, which over the years have added up to days, which are unaccounted for. Me and my cousins, we'll never know how we ended up in Michigan that time. But as far as anyone knows, no one has ever gotten hurt on my watch and nothing illegal ever went down."

I don't know if my neighbor's a salesman or not, but I am buying everything this guy's selling and I would go so far as to say that I would beat the crap out of anyone if I heard them tell him he's irresponsible. This is a man who knows what's up. "So that's what you want in life?" I find myself asking. "To have adventures? Do you want to have adventures with anyone in particular? Or raise any little adventurers? And if so, how many?" I reach for his whiskey glass, take a tiny sip of it, and then give it back to him. "Go on."

He laughs at me, ever so gently. Trevor used to get so judgmental whenever I drank, especially if we were at a nice restaurant or with his family. I guess I forgot that dates can be fun. With guys like Billy at least.

"Well," he says, "I actually do love kids."

"Yeah?"

"Yeah. I babysit for my brother and my cousins all the time. Whenever they let me, I mean. Yeah, I'd love to have kids of my own someday. I guess I always kind of assumed I'd have a bunch of kids at some point, in the same way I assumed I and everyone I knew would keep havin' fun forever..." He stares down into his glass, twirls the ice cubes around, and takes a sip. "I guess I thought that kind of stuff just happens. But then I saw my brother and my best friends—my cousins, those assholes—I saw how they had to work for it. Y'know? They kind of changed all of a sudden and they made a decision and all of a sudden they knew..."

"Knew what?"

"Who they wanted. What they wanted with her. And that they wanted it *now*. Not some hypothetical time in the future. And they wanted it forever. There was always a struggle, and then it got clear for them. And then it was like that's how it's always been. It's like they forgot the long and winding road, you know?"

I nod. I swear to God, if he starts singing a Beatles song, I'm dead.

"I mean, if I'm being honest, I do feel left out sometimes now. They give me shit—that's what we do, we give each other shit. But when I'm with my family, like at my grandad's birthday last week...I don't really feel so much like the last man standing so much as I feel like I'm that Sicilian guy who's always rolling the boulder up a hill by himself? Cicero?"

I smile at that. "Sisyphus. Greek."

"Yeah. Homer, right? Anyway, I guess when you get down to it, I'm just glad I was a part of that winding road they were on. And I want to end up where they are at the end of the day. Those are the people I love and respect the most. My grandparents and my parents and Nolan and Dec and Eddie—all those guys. I don't want to feel left behind. I think I'm just…" He finally looks up from the glass, glancing at me for one warm second. "I dunno. I know I'm a lot. But I think I got a lot to give someone. I just need that someone to believe I've got what it takes to be in a relationship enough for the both of us."

Well. Shit.

"Billy O'Sullivan," I say almost dreamily, even though I feel more awake than I've felt in years. "I am certain you will find someone who believes you've got what it takes." He looks so disappointed all of a sudden, I reach out to touch his hand, and he just stares at my hand until I take it away. "Here I thought you were a wiseass, but you are, in fact, a wise soul. With a good heart."

He opens his mouth to say something and then shuts it. He almost looks shy all of a sudden, which is not a look I ever thought I'd see on Billy Boston's face.

"What?" I ask. "What were you going to say?"

"Nothing—I was just gonna make a joke. But then I decided to take in what you said." He stares into his glass again, swirls the ice around again, and says, "Thank you. Coming from you, that means a lot. If you meant it."

"Of course I meant it."

"Cool. Well, I think you're all the good things too."

Why is that so cute? "Surely not *all* of them."

"All the ones I can think of. Probably a lot more." He places the tumbler down on the table as if it weighs a ton and then swipes his hand across his lips, looks at me, and says, "I think maybe you bring out the best in me, Red." Then he picks up the glass again and empties it into his mouth.

That mouth.

"Was that a line?" I instantly wish I hadn't asked because if it was, I don't think I want to know.

"I'm pretty sure I've meant everything I've ever said to you, Donna Fischer."

"A-plus" is all I have to say to that. "You know, at this point in a date, if things are going well, it's appropriate to reach across the table and hold your date's hand," I offer.

When he hesitates to reach for my hand, I say, "It's going well. Take my hand."

He does.

And I start leaning in for a kiss...but then Saverio and, like, a thousand other people who work here parade out of the kitchen. Saverio's holding one slice of cake with a sparkler on it, and he and the other servers are warming up and humming "Happy Birthday" to someone at a table near us. It's a table of ten people, and the birthday girl appears to be a lady in her late seventies.

Billy lets go of my hand, his full attention now given to the birthday girl—who, as far as I know, is a total stranger to him. He stands up and joins in the singing.

"*Happy birthday to youse!*" he yell-sings. "*Happy birthday toooo yooouuuuuse! Happy birthday, dear—*" He waits to hear the name of the person he's serenading. "*Robertaaaahhhhh! Happy wicked fuckin' awesome birthday toooo yoooouuuuuse!*" He claps—so loudly it startles me. "*Aaaaand many moooorrrrrre!*" he chants as he jogs over to her table, picks her up out of her chair, twirls her around, and dips her. Then he gives Roberta a big old wicked awesome surprising kiss on her chubby cheek.

I hold my breath as I wait to see if Billy's going to get slapped or not.

He doesn't get slapped.

Roberta is absolutely delighted by him, and it might be my imagination but it seems to me that her hand slips as she hugs him and clumsily grabs his butt under his suit jacket.

I join in the applause, of course. I am very happy for Roberta. Not super happy that Billy's pulled up a chair to join her at her table and she's feeding him a bite of her cake, though. Definitely not pleased that he seems to have completely forgotten me over here as he introduces himself to everyone else in her party.

I mean, it's charming. It's not like I don't appreciate his joie de vivre and his interest in other people. It's just that it has become clear to me that it doesn't take much to earn Billy Boston's attention. You just have to exist and be in front of him. So that's another note I can give him in the interest of teaching him how to hypothetically date someone.

And honestly, I'm a little relieved. Not hurt at all. Relieved. Because his charm was working on me. But now that I realize he makes these connections with *everyone*, my heart goes right back into its protective sleeve. We were connecting because that's what Billy does. There wasn't something special brewing between us. And that kind of connection is as fleeting as some of my relationships with my patients.

Here one minute.

Gone the next.

Like I said, I'm relieved. This means we can keep doing the no-strings thing until he gets himself a girlfriend. This means we aren't getting attached.

A minute or five later, after I've checked my texts and returned from the ladies room and stacked some of the plates on our table, Billy remembers I exist and comes back to join me.

"Okay, here's the deal. After-party at Roberta's

retirement community over in Brookline. They got a shuttle bus. Whaddya say? You can meet some potential clients."

"Actually, I think I'm gonna head home."

"What? Come on, it's only eleven."

"I know, but I have to work tomorrow, so..."

He looks disappointed. Not in me, in himself. And now I feel bad.

"But I had a really great time. Honestly. Thank you so much for a wonderful dinner. You did great." I give him a little kiss on the cheek as I get up, gathering my things.

He shrugs and scratches the back of his neck. "Yeah, well, thank *you*. I'll get the check and find that guy I hired to drive us home."

"I can just Uber home and come get my car in the morning—it's fine, really. Just let me know when you're free to help out at the house again. You should go hang out with your new friends."

"Absolutely not, young lady."

But I'm out the door before he can stop me. And I know he won't try to catch up with me either. Not because he isn't a gentleman. Because I think we both know we'd get pretty tangled up in strings if we get into the back seat of a car together tonight.

billy

BILLY BOSTON AND THE PRISONER OF ASS GRABBIN'

Knock, knock, knock.

I throw the wallpaper I just tore into the trash barrel I brought to Donna's house. I've been working here for the past hour, getting the lay of the land. There's some ugly here, some bad, but the bones are good, as they say.

Donna was supposed to meet me here about an hour ago. I've been texting her, but I didn't call because of the nature of her job, sometimes she has to stay late. I go to the front door and open it. And there she is, slightly out of breath, looking stressed but pretty as ever.

"You don't have to knock—it's your house," I say.

She puts her hands on her hips. "I gave you the keys."

"Well, I didn't lock it when I came in here."

99

"Oh. Well. Sorry I'm late."

"Don't worry about it. You want some good news? You look like you could use some good news."

"I could definitely use some good news."

"Come on in." I step down and hold the door open for her as she enters. My hand naturally finds the small of her back to guide her in. Completely unnecessary. But it feels good.

"It still looks like an awful lot of work to me," she says, her gaze roaming the house.

"Yeah, but let's focus on the good first. Here." I hold out my hands, presenting the area I was just working on. "I had a hunch that if I tore back this plasterboard..."

"Shiplap!" Donna says, full of wonder, like she's a little girl and I just presented her with a unicorn.

"Shiplap," I confirm with a nod. "Chicks still dig shiplap, right?"

Donna smiles the first smile I've seen on her since she got here. I'm gonna make sure it stays. "I can confirm that I will always love me some shiplap."

"Come on—there's more." I place my hand on the small of her back again as I guide her around the house. Yes, it desperately needs a reno. But there are bits and pieces that are unique and kind of amazing. There's one room stuffed with trash and furniture, but some of the furniture is really great and just needs a polish. And that room was once and will again be a beautiful three-season sunroom.

"It'll be gorgeous once it's cleared out and cleaned up," I say, guiding her to look past the trash to what it could be.

Donna sighs, but this time it's not stressed. It's well on its way to relaxed. "I see it. I do."

"Okay, last thing. Come down to the basement. I got somethin' wicked awesome to show you."

Donna rolls her eyes. "But I can see your penis so much better in this light."

I laugh. "That's not what I was gonna show you, but now that is definitely happening. Come on."

I take her hand and lead her to the entrance down to the basement. Because we're going down steep steps and even when the lights are on it's dark down there. That's why. It's not like I'm some cheeseball who can't stop touching her.

"There aren't any birds or blood water or any other crazy-scary stuff down here, is there?" Donna asks, the tension creeping back into her voice.

"I promise there's a good thing down here. And it's just a house, Donna." Most people think Boston is my native accent. It's not. It's Cocky. That's my true native tongue. And that's how I sound when I say it.

But that's for her benefit. Because it *was* strange when I arrived at the house. The air always feels strange and the light never seems like it matches the time of day. I wasn't exactly excited to explore this basement by myself.

But holding her hand now, I don't feel any of that. It's just a basement that's a little dark and not very airy, like any other basement.

"Billy, I can't see," Donna says, and I hear the panic rising in her voice.

"Babe, I got you." I flip on the lights. "There."

Donna squints and blinks her eyes a couple of times. It's still not nearly as bright as upstairs, but when her eyes do adjust, I watch her clock what I wanted to show her. It makes me smile.

"What am I looking at? Is that a cage for a serial killer to keep the women he kidnaps in?"

My smile fades fast. "What? No, it's a wine cellar."

"Oh!" Donna says in a much more chipper tone than when she was probably thinking her late patient was a serial killer. She walks into the little space. The racks are completely empty and there are bars everywhere, so I can see why she thought it was a cage. She looks up and down and around, but I can't read her expression.

I realize I don't know if she loves wine. I know she *likes* it. That's what she drinks at her apartment. It's what she asked for at the restaurant.

But what's her favorite? Red or white? Italian, French, Napa Valley? Does she even have a favorite?

Our date was wonderful. A little too wonderful.

I've never really opened up to a girl like that before. I always told my family there was this one girl but she couldn't handle me because I was too mysterious, but I've never gotten close enough for there to be "one girl." And it's not that they wouldn't want to be with me because I'm too mysterious—those girls have never been interested in me the way I am at home. The Billy that's relaxed. They want the Billy that they think only exists between the hours of 10:00 p.m. and 4:00 a.m. During a full moon.

Like a werewolf.

So it felt good to tell Donna those things about myself. Even though it wasn't a real date. I felt like I was really connecting with her. Which is not what I was supposed to feel. Which is why I jumped ship to the neighboring birthday party.

But it has made me curious about getting the same from her since the other night.

I want to know what makes Donna tick. But I'm not teaching *her* how to date. And nowhere is it written in the bylaws of our no-strings agreement that we can get to know each other as people. So I hid by creating a scene.

I've always been good at that. What am I saying? I'm the fucking best at it.

Donna puts her head in her hands and sighs. It's not the *I'm so relaxed and happy that I discovered I'm now the proud owner of a wine cellar* sigh. It's the sigh of someone so tired and stressed, they wouldn't mind being in a basement cage with a serial killer and put out of their misery.

"So, I guess you aren't a big fan of wine..." I say, because I don't know what else I'm allowed to say to her right now.

Donna removes her hands from her face and shakes her head. "No. I love wine. I certainly could use a glass right now." She places her hands on her hips and stares at the floor, a thousand miles into the Earth. "It was just a long day at work. Which made me late. I was even later because I was speeding."

I narrow my eyes. "Well, you did it wrong, then."

She gives me a look. "I mean I got pulled over. And I got a ticket. And I look at this wine cellar and I don't think, *Cool, I have a wine cellar.* I think about all the money I don't have to fill it with nice bottles of wine."

I want so badly to offer to fill it. And I don't mean that in the bad dirty joke way either. *For real* for real. She could have all my money if it would turn that sad sigh into a smile. I know I can't do that. I know she wouldn't accept it.

Doesn't mean I can't help some other way. "Give me the ticket."

"What? Why?"

"I'll take care of it, that's why."

Donna gives me a disapproving look. "I can afford to pay the speeding ticket. I'm not broke."

"I didn't say I'm going to pay it. I'm gonna take care of it." I shrug. "I know a guy."

Donna smiles a smile she clearly can't help, shaking her head because I'm so charming and surprising. My favorite kind of smile. "Of course you do."

I motion for her to give it to me, and she fishes the ticket out of her purse and hands it over.

She doesn't slow her momentum toward me; she wraps her arms around my neck. "Thank you." She tilts her chin up, and I get that kiss I wanted. Easily worth paying the state of Massachusetts a fine if my guy doesn't come through.

"You're welcome."

She gives me one of my other favorite looks. A look that says that kiss is only the start of what she wants from me. "It's been a long day. What do you say we play instead of working? Something where I don't have to think about anything. You decide. You're in charge."

It's an easy answer. An easy yes and the guarantee of a good time. Except I don't say yes. I've been addicted to Donna's body for a while now, needing my hit on a regular basis. But I'm starting to become addicted to helping her. I liked coming to the rescue and fixing her dishwasher. I like that I can take care of this ticket, help her relax, and make the house she inherited something great instead of a burden.

"How about we do both?" I say, and she immediately looks intrigued.

Knock, knock, knock.

I rap my nightstick against the bars of the wine cellar turned prison cell. And when I say nightstick, I do not mean my erection. Although I could absolutely knock on steel with my wood right now.

"On your feet, inmate," I bark. I'm now wearing blue dress pants, a blue button-down shirt, and I have a fake badge on my chest, real handcuffs hanging from my belt, and I've got a billy club. Just happened to have these in the trunk of my car.

My beautiful, indignant prisoner rises from the couch cushion I found. She's stripped down to plain white cotton panties and a ribbed white cotton tank top. Not because she had it as a costume in her car, but because tomorrow's her laundry day. Still, they look like prison-issue clothing to me.

I could have stripped her naked. I'm in charge of this prison after all. But then this would have been all role and no play because I wouldn't be able to stop myself from just skipping to the end and getting inside her. I'm hard enough watching her delicious ass rise, filling out those panties.

When she's standing in front of me, she folds her arms, which pushes up her tits, making her tank top even tighter and her hard nipples even clearer through the thin fabric. She levels me with a petulant stare. "The fuck do you want?"

"I'm gonna search your cell. Turn around and put your hands on the wall."

She scoffs but then complies, like she's a hardened criminal who's done this a thousand times before. She flattens her hands against the back wall, sticking her ass out on purpose.

I open the cell door and stalk inside, my boots making a satisfying, heavy thump with each step. I smack her ass.

"Hey! You can't do that. I have rights!"

I lean in, pressing my lips against her ear. "Not in here. In here, *this*"—I roughly palm her ass—"belongs to me." Donna's acting tough, but I hear the little gasp that's all pleasure.

"Spread your legs," I order. I tap the insides of both her legs to encourage her to spread them wider, and she does. I take a step back to admire her body, spread out just for me. I literally won the fucking lottery, but that didn't make me feel anywhere near as lucky as I feel in this moment, taking in this goddess who is now under my lock and key.

And now it is time for me to frisk her. I start with her tits—because why wouldn't I—massaging them for quite some time, just to be thorough. I move to the ass, because she could be hiding a lot of junk in there —more than just the hot flesh and muscle and fat that drives me out of my goddamn mind. And then a gentle caress of her pussy to make sure there are no weapons in there, aside from the wet warmth and taste that can bring me to my knees. Back to her ass, and then I massage her tits again—because I need to protect myself.

I'm guessing this is not proper procedure, but the whole time Donna's moaning and my cock, which was already hard, is now threatening to break out of the prison of my dress pants.

"I thought you were here to search my cell. Not me." Donna's trying to sound pissed off, but she's too turned on. No formal acting training.

I take her right wrist, hold it behind her back and lock the cuff around it. "I have to make sure you don't have anything dangerous on you first. Since you're such a bad girl."

I take her left wrist and lock the other cuff on it. Then I grab her arm and spin her around.

"I'm innocent, you jackass," she exhales. But she stares at me with dangerous, lust-filled eyes.

"The fuck you are," I growl. I drag her out of the dungeon cellar, her hands cuffed behind her back, in stark contrast to my put-together, powerful frame and costume. Donna's a strong woman. She has to be, given her job. So it means a lot that she would trust me enough to give me all this power over her. It turns me on, of course. But it also makes me feel something else that I'm not going to think about. Because I already feel like I'm losing control of my feelings while having control over her body.

I bring her to a chair in the middle of the basement. It feels dark and dangerous. But it's not the house creating that feeling. It's us, and we're playing with it.

"Don't you move," I growl into her ear.

She shivers but manages to frown up at me. "Fuck you."

I rise and pretend I'm giving her "cell" the once-over. But of course I'm just staring at my gorgeous jailbird the whole time.

I march back over. Slowly, so she can hear my heavy footsteps but can't see me. I swing myself around to face her in the chair, towering over her. "You're gonna tell me what I wanna know."

"The hell I am," Donna says with a smirk.

I fist her hair, giving it a gentle yank. A delighted gasp escapes her lips. "Oh yes, you are. By the time I'm done with you, you're gonna be beggin' me to put you back in that cell."

"Big talk," she mutters.

It's my turn to smirk. I let go of her hair. She's probably expecting me to spank her. But I go the opposite way. I kiss the spot on her neck that I know drives her wild. My eyes are closed, but I hear her pull at her cuffs. "Not fair," she whines.

"Don't care."

I work my way down, kissing her over her tank top. Lower and lower until I reach her slit, clearly visible through the wet spot on her panties. I kiss it. Once. Twice. Inhale. Breathing in Donna. My prisoner.

I stop pleasuring her with my mouth, suddenly pulling back.

She pulls at her cuffs again.

"You're gonna tell me what I want to know."

She doesn't nod in affirmation. Just bites her bottom lip. Which is good enough for me.

"Where are you from?"

"The moon."

I pinch a nipple, startling her.

"Jamaica Plain!" she answers again.

"Did I stutter? I didn't ask where you lived before you got locked up. Where did you grow up?" I look her in the eye. I'm sure my eyes are as hazy with lust as hers are, but I can see her realizing that I'm not asking about the criminal character she's pretending to be. I'm asking about Donna, my neighbor and no-strings girl.

"That's against the rules—"

I pinch the other nipple.

She squirms, the cuffs preventing her from moving too much in her chair. "I'm from Philadelphia."

I reward her answer with my mouth to her pussy. If I thought she was wet before, her panties are flooded now. "Why did you move to Boston?" I ask between kisses on her mound, over the very wet cotton.

"Because the guys in Boston are stupid and they're easy marks," Donna the criminal quips.

Oh, Donna. Poor Donna. Forced to wear panties and a tank top that's now property of the Billy Boston Department of Erections. But that means they're mine to do with as I please.

I grab the left side of her panties, tear, and then rip them. I do the same to the right. I pull the tatters out from under her and ball them up. "These can go in your mouth if you're not going to answer my questions."

Donna's breathing like she's been running a marathon, even though she's been chained in a chair for the last few minutes. "I followed my high school boyfriend to Boston for college. It was really hard to leave, because my oma and opa are there and I didn't want to leave them. But even after my ex left, I decided to stay because I got a lot of good job offers. And because I fell in love with Boston. It was a hard choice, but I made it."

Boston the city. *She fell in love with Boston the* city.

"But fuck you," she adds.

All right. I return to her pussy, all bare and slick. I kiss her clit and place my hands on her thighs, encouraging her to spread wider so I can lick her. With each lick I increase the pressure little by little. And with each lick Donna tilts her pelvis forward just a little bit more. When I can't press my tongue any harder and she can't rock forward any farther without falling off the chair, I stiffen my tongue and fuck her with it, as deep as I can go. That's when Donna cries out. No holding back. No neighbors to worry about.

"Oh God. Oh God. *Biiiiiilllyyyy!*" She chants and moans, bucking and thrashing as much as she can in her position. I keep going until she comes all over my face.

Finally I pull back, with a very satisfied grin as I wipe my face, savoring the hard evidence I got out of my little prisoner. I got what I wanted. Donna is limp in the chair, a sated grin on her pretty lips. Lips I intend to put to work.

My smile vanishes as I realize something. Something very distressing and important. "Wait, are you a Philly Lightning fan?"

She nods slowly, her sated grin turning evil.

Oh, hell no.

I pick her up swiftly. She's been acting pretty tough up until this point, but she lets out a fun little squeal. I sit down in the chair and place her over my knee, spanking her three times.

"Why was it hard to decide to stay in Boston? Philly's a city for dirtbags."

"They say the same about you."

"Yeah, that's what dirtbags think. They think non-dirtbags are dirtbags to hide from their own dirtbaginess."

"Fuck you," she says, but she's laughing.

I fist her hair and spank her some more.

I ask Donna more questions, spanking her when she's sassy and rubbing her tits when I like the answer. I learn that she's an only child and her parents divorced when she was thirteen. She's always been close to her oma and opa and they've always celebrated Oktoberfest. She loves German beer.

I'm beyond horny for her body, but now I'm just as lustful for who she is. I try not to make the interrogation too heavy. So I also get her favorite color— crimson red, which is acceptable because it's one of the Boston Tomcats team colors—and her dream vacation, which is to see the northern lights in Norway.

When her ass is nice and pink, she begs, "I'll be good! Please, sir, I'll suck your cock. No more spanking."

I'm used to seeing Donna all feisty, so this sudden turn makes me a little nervous, despite hearing the four words any straight man would die to hear this woman say to him. "You remember the safe word?"

She looks back at me like I'm an idiot. "Of course. Did I use it? Did I stutter?" *There she is.*

That earns her four more swats on her ass, two on each cheek.

"Just for that, the new safe word is *the Philly Lightning suck* instead of *the New York Rebels suck*."

"I mean, those are safe *words*, but whatever floats your boat."

I growl and lift her up, throwing her over my shoulder. I quickly search for what I'm looking for and find a blanket that will work. I fold it up and place it on the ground in front of the chair. Then I lower Donna to her feet, but her legs are wobbly from all the pleasure and punishment, so I hang on to her lightly for support. "On your knees, inmate," I say, my voice low and dangerous.

"Yes, sir," Donna says obediently, making *my* knees weak. Then she smirks; the little minx knows exactly what she's doing to me. She drops to her knees on top of the folded blanket, and I take a seat in the chair.

"This would be a lot easier if my hands weren't cuffed, sir," she says, leaning to one side and moving her arms to the other side behind her, jangling the cuffs to emphasize her point. She pouts adorably.

"Yeah, probably would be. But we like things *hard* around here." I unbuckle my belt, unbutton and unzip my pants, and pull out my aching cock myself. It's dripping with precum. Donna's eyes grow wide, and she bites her bottom lip in that way that drives me absolutely insane. "Get to work, inmate."

Donna licks her lips and kisses the head of my cock. I close my eyes and groan, throwing my head back, the pleasure already almost too much to handle.

"Donna..." I whisper. We forgot to give each other character names, but fuck it.

"Yes, sir? What can I do for you?" She makes clear her question is rhetorical by licking my shaft from base to tip—slowly. So slowly. She's torturing me now. She's on her knees, cuffed, and I'm a prisoner to her mouth. When she reaches the tip, she takes me into her mouth. As much as she can. My eyes jolt open and I bolt upright. She starts sucking intensely, deep throating, never letting my cock out of her mouth because she wouldn't be able to place it back in without the use of her hands. I don't know how to stop myself from coming in that sweet mouth. I need to be inside her pussy before I do.

"Stop," I say weakly. She ignores me. "Stop," I mutter again. She still doesn't.

I fist her hair, forcing her head back. It's wicked frustrating to put an end to the pleasure she was giving me, but my cock falls out of her mouth with a satisfying wet *pop*.

"I said stop, inmate." My chest is heaving.

She gives me a knowing smile, her lipstick smeared and strands of hair plastered to her forehead. "Did you say your safe words? *The Boston Tomcats suck*?"

That does it. I take the scoop of her tank top in my hands and rip it apart, exposing her gorgeous breasts. I take out the condom I put in my pants pocket and stand up, rolling it on in front of her.

"You are my prisoner. Your body is mine. You have no control. And my cock is going in your pussy."

"Understood, sir," she says, a wide smile on her face.

I can't help the smile that spreads across mine. It's not in character at all, but fuck it. Once the condom is on I sit back down, pull her up onto my lap, and guide her pussy down to my cock. It's awkward as fuck on the chair, with her hands cuffed. But we make it work. I thrust up into her, and she grinds her hips as I do. She arches back, and I lick and kiss and suck her tits, and we only last a few minutes before we're both coming.

I cover her mouth with my hand. We're alone, far away from anyone who could hear her. But I want her to feel like she's mine, just for a moment. She's chained up, filled with me, and I'm in control. Which means I'll take care of her. She screams her pleasure and the frustration of her day into the palm of my hand, and I follow right behind her, chanting her name as my orgasm racks my body.

It takes some time for me to be able to move again. Without making her get up, I manage to pick up the pants from around my ankles, fish the keys out of the pocket, and uncuff her. She was struggling a lot and she wore them for a long time, so there are some pretty serious ligature marks on her wrists. Her tank top's all torn up; her panties are ripped up on the floor. Did I go too far?

"I'm so sorry," I tell her. And I really am. I feel like I failed her. This is what I do. I take things too far. This is why I'm gonna die alone. I kiss her wrists. And I don't plan to stop kissing them until those red marks go away.

Donna shakes her head vehemently. "Do. Not. Be. Sorry. Really. That was thrilling. Right?"

"Yes, ma'am." Still, I kiss her wrists. She is strong. But I was supposed to protect her. "Why are you so into role-play anyway?" I don't look at her when I ask. Just continue to kiss her wrists.

"Because it's fun. Right?"

"Is this how you do it with other guys or just me?"

She doesn't answer, and I didn't expect her to. I keep kissing her wrists.

"You're more fun than other guys," she finally says. "We're just having fun."

I look up at her. She looks at me. Her words sounded so certain, but there's something in her eyes. Like she's really asking me.

"Yeah. This is fun. Keeps things fun and easy." I shrug.

The lights start flickering. There's buzzing and zapping and then they just turn off for a second. Then they come back on, still flickering. Donna's no longer in a dreamy state. "What the hell?"

And then all of a sudden an old radio that's in a pile in a corner turns on. There's static and screeching and then it goes to really loud, creepy classical music. Like that "Something Wicked This Way Comes" song from a Harry Potter movie.

Donna stares at me, wide-eyed and trembling. I can tell she's so freaked out she can't even form words.

"Uh. Well. I never got around to giving you the bad news. It seems like the electrical and the plumbing needs work," I tell her in my native cocky tongue. But I don't mean it. The electrical panel looked fine when I checked it. It was obviously upgraded. The plumbing looked fine too, for the most part. But it has to be an old-house thing, or I have no idea why this is happening, unless there's a storm out there all of a sudden.

"Oh. Well..." Donna's voice rises in panic. "Anyway, I wouldn't just role-play with anyone. I like role-playing with you. You're good at it." She tries to play it off like she isn't scared, just continuing our conversation from earlier.

I follow her lead. "Oh, yeah, me too. I like doing this with you a lot too." And though we're not as relaxed as we were before, it felt better to say that than blowing this off as something that's no big deal.

"And if you really want to know," she continues, "I do it because my job is stressful. And sad. And sometimes I just want to get off work and be someone else. Someone who doesn't have to deal with all the things I deal with every day. While having orgasms. More bang for my buck. You know?"

"Understood."

And just as suddenly as it turned on, the radio shuts off.

But the damn lights are still flickering.

After a few seconds, Donna laughs. I laugh. We're both laughing at how totally absurd this situation is, I think.

"So can we start work on this place tomorrow? I got the day off."

"Sure, yeah. Oh, wait. Shit. My cousin's niece Piper is flying in from New York tomorrow. I gotta look after her for the day."

"Oh." Donna says. "Wait, so she's not *your* niece?"

"Nope. She's my cousin's wife's niece. I don't think there's a word for that. All I know is we're not related by blood, which is good because she's always checking out our butts—me and my cousins—and we have to pretend that she isn't."

Donna laughs really hard at that. Which is very strange because it's not funny. "How do you know?"

"She's been checking out our butts since she was, like, thirteen! Do you know how bad kids are at hiding things?"

That just makes her laugh harder. Which is even stranger. I guess she was more freaked out by the radio thing than I was.

She climbs off me and uses the blanket to wipe us both off. "So, is there a butt convention in Boston that I don't know about? What's she coming to town for?"

I pull my pants back up and go get Donna's clothes to bring to her. "Uh, some kind of author thing. She got a ticket to go to a reading or something at Harvard. Her parents and my cousin are busy, so I offered to be her chaperone. She'll only be here for a few hours after the reading, but I'm not sure what to do with her after. She's almost seventeen. Should I take her to the zoo? Or one of those tea rooms with those little round French cookies in different colors that girls freak out about?"

Donna starts getting dressed, minus undergarments, and now she's laughing in a totally different way. Like she's amused. She's all glassy eyed when she looks at me. "That is adorable. But more appropriate for a seven-year-old. If she's almost seventeen and lives in New York and going to author events, then she's probably pretty mature. I bet she'd enjoy hanging out around Harvard."

"There are so many college guys' butts around

there, though. I don't think I can beat up every single one of them if they try to hit on her."

That makes Donna snort-laugh. Which is very satisfying. Except I wasn't kidding. And the thing is I'm realizing that I really want Donna to come with me. I think I just really want Donna.

Suddenly the lights stop flickering.

Suddenly I know what I have to do. I can't just ask Donna out yet because it'll scare her off. I have to *trick* Donna into thinking she's still teaching me how to date someone else when really I'm *treating* her to dates with me. I'll learn how to date *her*, and she'll figure out eventually that it's not that scary to be in a real relationship with me. Everybody wins.

The light overhead buzzes and then goes off and on again.

I guess I will have to call in an electrician.

"So listen, I've never been alone with Piper and I have no idea what to talk to her about. Since you got the day off tomorrow, why don't you come with me to hang with her? You can teach me how to behave in case I end up dating a single mom with a teenage daughter. Plus you can help me take on those preppy trust-fund assholes who try to chat her up." I hold my breath waiting for her response.

I watch a million conflicting microexpressions flicker across her face. Is she flattered? Is she disappointed? Is she offended? I've been inside this woman so many times, but I never feel like I can get inside her head.

Finally she says, "Oh. Yeah. I mean, I was just going to do laundry and clean up around here and look at paint colors, but...I have a little less laundry to do now, thanks to you, so..."

"I will purchase replacements for you immediately."

"Not necessary."

"They're standard issue, inmate. I *will* purchase replacements for you immediately," I repeat.

She laughs and gives in, and I silently hope that I will have many more opportunities to tear up those replacements again.

EIGHT

donna

PIPER-HORMONAL ACTIVITY

I've seen a lot of different versions of my neighbor. Most recently he's been a plumber, a Mark Wahlberg, and a corrections officer. Some all-time favorite roles he's played with me in private include, but are not limited to, New Orleans Vampire Billy, Grumpy English Professor Billy, and Brokenhearted Strip Club Client Billy. If I'm being honest, I also very much enjoyed First Date Billy.

But today I'm seeing him in a very different kind of role—one that does not involve sex. At all. Today I'm witnessing Overprotective Sort-of Uncle Billy who will cut anyone with a penis if he even looks at his cousin's wife's niece. When we picked her up from the airport, a male flight attendant accompanied Piper to the Arrivals pickup area and this man was clearly gay, but as soon as they walked through the doors, Billy got up in that flight attendant's face and said, "Okay, I'll take it from here, hotshot. This is not *that* kind of pickup area, you understand? Move it along."

He walks alongside her like he's Secret Service and she's a head of state.

The head of the state of virginity, that is.

I mean, this girl is adorable. She isn't seventeen yet, and she does not strike me as someone who's ready to be sexually active, as much as her hormones seem to be telling her otherwise. But the way Billy is being overprotective of her and cockblocking any guy who tries to talk to her, you'd think she's twelve.

This is the opposite of the Billy who was spanking me in a basement yesterday, but it's so cute and I can't help but find it endearing.

And Piper is so cute. She has long, dark brown hair with bangs, black-rimmed glasses, and the wide, innocent eyes of a doe—if that doe was super into hot guys' butts. She's wearing a sweater and wool coat with a plaid miniskirt and thick black tights. She's carrying a huge weekender bag around even though she isn't staying the night, but she brought three big hardcover books by her favorite romantasy author. Because romantasy is a thing now, I guess?

I can't tell if she's more excited that she got one of her favorite authors to sign her books at the reading or that she's in Cambridge, surrounded by young men in jeans, blazers, and peacoats. But if I could be even ten percent as excited about anything as she is about everything, it would be so much easier to face each day.

While she was attending the ticketed event in a theater, Billy and I waited for her in the tiny lobby. Not because she asked us to and not because people are allowed to loiter in the small lobby. Because Billy wanted to be there to rescue Piper in case there was a fire or a really good-looking drunk Harvard guy hitting on her during the daytime literary event.

It was the most time I've ever spent with him without talking. I mean, not counting the times I've had his cock in my mouth. He had zero chill as he sat there, probably imagining a bunch of trust-fund guys gangbanging her during the reading or something. I honestly don't know what he thought would happen in there, but he was very relieved to see her walking out, finally, with a huge smile on her sweet face and her arms around three books instead of frat boys.

Now we're walking through Harvard Square, down the brick-paved sidewalks, to a bar that Billy says he worked at "five or ten years ago" so he knows the owner and can get Piper in to drink hot chocolate. Did I calmly mention to him that if he were, in fact, dating a single mom it would not be a great idea to take her underage daughter to a bar, even though he's only going to buy her hot chocolate? I did. Do I think Piper is going to love going to a bar in Harvard Square and wish I had a sort-of-uncle like Billy when I was growing up? I do. Piper's going to have so much to brag about with her friends.

And honestly, I'm happy because I can't remember the last time I just walked around on a day off. It's my favorite month and it's a beautiful, crisp fall day. The leaves are changing, it's boot season, and everything smells like pumpkin spice. Harvard Square is vibrant and bustling and almost has as much energy as Piper when she's explaining her favorite book series to us.

"So, book one is called *Riders of Storm and Fire* and it's an epic, spicy story centered on a group of dragon riders—mainly Zephyr and Ember. There's a movie in development, and it will go into production next year! They still haven't found a young actor swoony enough to play Zephyr, because Zac Efron is too old now, unfortunately. I'm going as Ember for Halloween and I have an orange wig—not natural red like your hair, but like the color of cartoon fire, if you know what I mean."

"I do, and that will look hot with your complexion."

She blushes. "I guess."

"She wears pants, right? Ember wears baggy pants and a long, heavy sweater?" Billy asks, but he's really telling her.

"They're pants, yeah, but they're really tight, like the sweater."

"Absolutely not, young lady."

She rolls her eyes at him. "Dragon riders have to wear tight clothes because of the wind."

"Obvi. Keep telling us about Zephyr and Ember," I say, while narrowing my eyes at Billy.

"OMG, Zephyr is so hot. He's six foot five and has long wavy chestnut-brown hair and ocean eyes with flecks of silver. He has a strong yet lean build with rippling muscles. He is very calm and broody and analytical but also a total badass when it comes to protecting the people he cares about. He's an alpha in the streets *and* the sheets! Not OTT alpha, though, and the balance of power between him and Ember is chef's kiss!"

"Nice," I say, even though I have no idea what OTT means.

"Sounds like a dick to me," Billy mutters. "And if he's six foot five why isn't he playing basketball instead of riding a dragon? I don't trust this guy. He makes bad life choices."

"Billy!" I hiss.

"And Ember is really passionate and brilliant when it comes to riding and understanding her dragon. There's so much tension and banter between her and Zephyr at first and then so much mutual respect, and they just struggle so much with their loyalty to their factions and their growing attraction to each other!" Piper looks like she's about to burst into flames as she hugs her bag full of books to her chest.

"Sounds delicious."

"What are you lookin' at?" Billy says to a couple of undergrad guys who pass by. "She's sixteen—keep movin'!"

I keep glancing over at Piper when he does this, to see if she's horrified or embarrassed, and it looks to me like she's just used to it. She must have a lot of men in her family looking out for her. She just turns her head to check out those guys' butts as they walk away. "Anyway, I can't believe I finally got to meet Rachel Balfour. She was so friendly for someone who hates New Yorkers for sports reasons."

"Hey, that is an excellent reason to hate New Yorkers," Billy says as he keeps his eye on a forty-year-old man who's walking toward us. "I hate all New Yorkers except the ones I'm related to. And even they're assholes. Except you, Piper. And Maddie and Cora. And your mom. Am I related to her too? I can't keep track."

"Thanks. And I guess so, but my mom's super basic, so it doesn't matter."

"Okay, we're here." Billy stops in front of an Irish dive bar and opens the door for us. "Don't make eye contact with any of the guys in here except me," he says to Piper. "You got it?" Then he looks at me. "Same goes for you, young lady." He winks.

I gotta say, the wink really does it for me. "Absolutely not, young man" is my reply.

The place is pretty busy for a Saturday afternoon. Decorated for Halloween and blaring country music from a jukebox. It's an Irish pub, but it's still hard to imagine Billy working here. Why an Irish pub in Harvard Square of all places, when he could have worked at one in any Boston neighborhood? He is just full of surprises. I mean, the guy drives a Volvo, for crying out loud, which is pretty much the last kind of vehicle I'd expect him to drive. If he told me he drove a parade float everywhere I'd be less surprised.

Billy walks into the pub like he owns the place. I now think this is probably how he walks into every place. He does some crazy handshake with an elderly man behind the bar, who is perhaps the actual owner, leans in to chat with him, gets a nod, then waves Piper and me over. "Have a seat, ladies." He gestures for Piper to sit at one of the empty barstools, and I take a seat next to her while Billy encourages a couple of college guys to move away from the bar and sit at a table that has just opened up.

Then he places his jacket over the stool next to Piper, goes behind the bar, rolls up his sleeves, and gets to work. "Okay, I ordered us some finger food. Virgin hot chocolate for the lovely young lady from the town with the Football Team Who Shall Not Be Named. And what can I make for the lovely young lady from the other town with the Other Football Team Who Shall Not Be Named?"

"Surprise me," I say, because I know he will.

"You got it. One summer snow comin' right up." He grins. "Bourbon smash with a little somethin' special I think you'll like."

Billy pours fresh mint and sliced grapefruit in a glass. Where he got these things from I do not know. Doesn't seem like that type of bar. But Billy makes things happen. He takes the muddler and gives it a little twirl, making sure I get a real good look at his hands and catching my eye with another wink. We both smile. Then he's all business, gently crushing the mint and grapefruit. The fragrance reaches my nostrils, all sweet and fresh, and I take a deep breath in. It's just wonderful.

Next, he scoops in some crushed ice, slamming it hard and making a sound like cymbals crashing. He reaches for the Elijah Craig Single Barrel, spinning the bottle before pouring a generous measure over the ice. The amber liquid seeps down in an artistic pattern, mixing with the frozen aromatics.

He caps the glass with a shaker tin and gives it a solid pump. Vigorous enough for me to get the idea but not so sexy that Piper gets any ideas whatsoever. The ice clinks like high hat drums. Even when he isn't moving his lips, Billy gets his point across loudly.

When the concert is over, he strains it all into a

rocks glass filled with fresh ice and garnishes it with a sprig of mint and another grapefruit slice, perched right on the rim. Last but not least, he grabs a little electric fan they've got on the bar. He takes a handful of powdered sugar and aims the fan at his open palm. The powdered sugar sprinkles down upon the glass and garnish, making it look like it's been kissed by frost.

"What the fuck, buddy?" We all turn to find that a middle-aged man standing next to us is also freshly dusted with sugar snow.

"Sorry, man. Your drinks are on me," Billy tells him amiably.

"Fuckin' A," says the happy snowman, raising his glass in salute.

"And there you are, madam. One summer snow." He slides the drink across the counter.

Piper applauds as I take a sip. "Oh, that's delicious," I tell him.

"Good. Hey, you got a little sugar...right...here." He wipes the corner of my mouth with his thumb and then sucks the tip of his thumb.

His eyes go a little wide. He's probably worried he's being too suggestive in front of his cousin's wife's niece. Good thing she's totally distracted by a preppy Harvard type who's walking past us up to the bar. She gives the back of his dark jeans a real good once-over.

Billy does not like that. But then the preppy guy gives Piper the up-down.

Billy's eyes look like they're burning so hot they're going to melt.

"Stella Artois," Preppy Guy says, not looking at Billy because he's grinning at Piper.

"Oh, you don't want a Stella Artois," Billy says.

That earns Billy the preppy guy's attention. "I don't?"

Billy shakes his head. "Nah, too simple."

He grabs a beer glass and pours Stella into it. I expect him to do a crappy pour and leave it all foamy with a ton of head. But Billy takes as much care with it as he did my drink. When he's done, Billy slides it toward Preppy.

Preppy looks at Billy, bewildered. "That's not Stella Artois?"

"Nah, man. The secret is in the garnish. Oh right, I forgot." Billy searches beneath the bar. "Where's my cocktail stick? Oh yeah, here it is." He pulls the baseball bat from beneath the bar and brandishes it at the preppy guy. "That's a Stella *Au Revoir*. As in sayonara and get the fuck outta here and quit eyeballin' underage girls!"

The preppy guy grabs the beer before hauling off, but Billy hops the counter and chases after him, yelling that he's also not going to take any shit from the guy's friends.

Left alone, Piper turns to me. "So, how long have you and Billy been seeing each other?"

"Oh, we aren't...I mean we aren't really dating. We just... We hang out sometimes. We've been neighbors for a couple of years, I guess? He's helping me fix up a house that I'm hoping to move into eventually."

"Really?! Is he doing, like, carpentry work and stuff?"

"Not yet, but maybe. We haven't quite started yet, but there's...a lot to do. And we keep getting sidetracked."

"Oh, *really*?" she says, waggling her eyebrows, just like Billy sometimes does. "How so?"

Wow, I am not going to get into it. So instead, I find myself blurting out, "I think the house might be haunted."

Piper puts down her mug of hot chocolate. "No way! By a ghost or a demon?"

"Ghost. Not a demon. It doesn't feel evil, it feels sad. And maybe frustrated. Sometimes angry. It might be my patient. Or his wife. Or someone who died on the property before my patient bought it—who knows. I don't know."

"Well, you need to find out. You need to ask who it is and what it wants."

I laugh. I love how this girl isn't hesitant about anything. "Just ask it, huh?"

"Well, you'll probably have to do a séance."

"Like, hire a medium?"

"No, you can use a Ouija board! We did it at my friend Shoshanna's sleepover once, and we contacted the spirit of a man who died in her building. It was kind of creepy but also cool."

"And you believe you actually contacted a spirit? You don't think anyone was messing around?"

"Oh, it was real. If any of us were messing around we would have pretended to conjure up a hot dead guy. This one was old and kind of mean, but not in a scary way. He was just really mad that his apartment, the one Shoshanna lives in, had been totally gutted. And that the Rebels traded his favorite player."

Billy's back behind the bar, and this gets his attention. "If he was a Rebels fan, then he was not to be trusted. There's no ghost at that house, just bad wiring." A guy nearby starts to tell Piper that he also used a Ouija board at a party once, but Billy holds his finger up to his face. "You are not a part of this conversation, Scooby-Doo. Move along."

"Well." Piper shrugs. "You should figure it out one way or another before you move in, right? Donna wouldn't have brought it up if she wasn't really wondering about it."

This girl is eerily astute.

"Can't hurt to have a séance," she tells me. "Just don't do it alone. You aren't supposed to do it with less than two people, so make sure Billy's with you.

And do it on the night of a full moon if you can. Or on Halloween or November first, because that's Samhain and that's when the barriers between the physical and spiritual worlds break down. Oh, and keep a lot of salt handy in case you contact a demon." She laughs. "I learned that from *Supernatural*. I don't know if it really helps to protect you, but I would do literally anything Dean Winchester told me to do."

"I don't like the sound of that guy either," Billy says. "But he has a cool name."

"Oh, also," Piper adds, tapping her chin. "There's always a chance one of you might get possessed by the spirit during the séance, but *don't* worry, it's only temporary. You'll need to draw a pentagram on the floor, with chalk, and make a protective circle before you start—to banish any negative entities." She says this like she's explaining how to use a hairdryer or something. "If you give me your number, I'll text you everything you need to know!"

"Okay." I tune out Billy, who's telling all the guys around us to back off while Piper and I get our phones out. The truth is I've been around dying and dead people for years as part of my job. I know what they tell me and I know that I've felt it when people's spirits pass out of their bodies. I don't know how else to explain what happens. I don't go around thinking about what happens to spirits that don't move on to some great beyond because I'm too busy trying to keep people comfortable while they're alive.

But what if that's what happened to Lars? Or his wife? What if they need my help? If he trusted me enough to leave me this property that meant so much to him, then I owe it to him to at least make sure I'm doing all I can for him. Or for her. I just hope it's Lars and not his wife, because from the way he described her she sounded kind of melodramatic. *And* a redhead. Which is a terrible combination.

And after seeing how protective Billy is of Piper, he's the only person I'd want around if I actually do a séance...

So far, being a homeowner isn't nearly as fun as I thought it would be.

piper

Dear Super-Secret Diary,

You will never guess where I am RN. Okay, I'll tell you! I'm on a plane, from Boston back to New York. As a very mature unaccompanied minor! First class! There's a guy on this flight who looks like a young Jensen Ackles. His dimples are a ten. His butt is a TEN. But he also has a girlfriend with him who is a ten... Sad trombone. Still, I had the most amazing trip, and I will write about most of it in my other journal, because, tragically, the true story of my trip to Harvard is PG-13 enough for my snooping mom to read about. My aunt's husband's cousin turned out to be a very responsible one-day guardian in his own way. I can't tell if Declan will be relieved or annoyed to learn this, LOL. I truly thought that Billy would be the one guy in my extended family who wouldn't do his best to ensure that I remain a virgin for the rest of my life.

And yet he did his best.

At least his best was fun. What was really fun, though, was meeting the future Mrs. Boston. LOL. I have a total girl crush on her, but it was so cute to watch her and Billy and how they'd watch each other when they thought the other wasn't looking—but I was looking. I have a new OTP, and I still have a swoony contact high from being around them. I am totally inspired, and that is why I have to write about it immediately!!!

Good Will Ghost Hunting

Everyone in his family had a theory as to why William O'Sullivan was still single. The Cannavale and the Cassidy and the O'Sullivan men all had one thing in common— amazing butts. And most of them had something else in common now too—amazing wives. All except for Billy. The theory among most of his relatives was that he was too busy having fun to have a girlfriend.

For Billy O'Sullivan was not just good at having fun— he was a wicked awesome genius when it came to shenanigans. To him it was an art, a science, and a way of life. He was always coming up with new equations for fun. If there was a seemingly unsolvable party problem, Billy could solve it.

Everyone's getting tired and morose? Crank up the air-conditioning and the Meat Loaf songs!

Rental company didn't deliver the bouncy castle? We're goin' to Walmart to get a big tent and a large inflatable bed—gather all the pillows you can find!

He knew all the equations, and he'd write them on his mirror in erasable pen when he couldn't sleep: Guinness plus whiskey plus Cannavale cousins plus Nolan plus Chumbawamba equals multiple unaccounted for hours and hundreds of question marks the next day.

Thanksgiving plus toilet plus firecracker equals urban legend.

But ironically, he did not understand the most important equation of all: Billy plus Donna equals true love forevah and evah. *Because he did not realize that he loved her and that she loved him. He had no idea how romantic he actually was. He was, in fact, troubled by what he perceived as a lack of romantic instincts.* Oh, will I, William O'Sullivan, ever get my HEA? Will I? *he found himself wondering.* "Have I wasted too much of my life partyin'? And will I nevah find myself a bride because of this?" *He'd become haunted by these questions, one might say.*

But he would eventually find the answer to his HEA problem, and Donna would be both his teacher and his solution.

One night—a night that was seemingly just like every other—he went to a Harvard bar with his buddy Murphy.

"Where should we park my car when we go to the Harvard bar?" Billy asked his friend. "Just kiddin'! We're takin' the T 'cause we're gonna get hammered!"

The place they went to was much like any other dive bar around Boston. Except that Murphy quickly spotted a wicked hot, curvaceous, and very smart redhead at the end of the bar counter. "Whoa," he said. "I'm goin' in." He smoothed down his gelled hair and sauntered over, in his tracksuit, to where the lady was sitting by herself.

"Oh, hello there," he said when she finally noticed him.

"Oh, hello," she said politely.

"My name is Murphy," he said, feigning a classy air. "What might your name be?"

"My name is Donna," she said, shaking his outstretched hand.

"Donna, Donna, Donna, yeah. I thought I recognized you," Murphy said. "I think we had a class together last semester."

"Oh yeah?" she said, playing along. "Which one?"

"Yeah, Theory of Love, I think it was. I sat behind ya."

Donna continued to politely chat with this fellow because she was a nice person—not because she was into Murphy.

But then a snobby Harvard student with thin blond hair that he wore in a ponytail came over with his equally snobby pals. "Excuse me," Ponytail Guy said to Murphy, even though he was not being polite. "What class did you say you were in with Donna? Theory of Love, you said?"

"Yep, that was it. Don't wanna brag, but I got an A."

"Did you? Well, then you must be well versed in all the major theories of love. Perhaps you could enlighten us about Gary Chapman's theory of the Five Love Languages?"

Murphy clearly had no idea what Ponytail Guy was talking about. "Uh, yeah, sure. There's, uh, Baby Talk, Dirty Talk, Filthy Talk..."

Ponytail and all his dumb friends laughed at him—and not in the good way.

"Oh, why don't you just go away," Donna said to Ponytail.

But then Billy walked right up to Ponytail, because loyalty was one of Billy's Top Five Greatest Attributes, after Awesome Butt, Boston Accent, Charming Grin, Genius of Fun, and Nice Hairy Chestiness—oh wait, that's Top Six. "Naw, naw, let's talk about marriage counselor and internationally best-selling author Gary Chapman, PhD, and his theory of the Five Love Languages," Billy said to Ponytail, getting all up in his boring face. "You wanna talk about his trademarked Acts of Service, Receiving Gifts, Quality Time, Words of Affirmation, or Physical Touch? Or would you like to also include the two recent additional love languages coined by dating site eHarmony—Shared Experiences and Emotional Security? Maybe you'd like to enlighten us about the Triangular Theory of Love, courtesy of Robert J. Sternberg?"

"Of course," said Ponytail. "You're speaking of Intimacy, Passion, and Decision slash Commitment."

"Yeah. I am. And you're speaking of words you memorized for an exam. You're about as passionate as my left shoe. Not the right one, though, because that one is wicked passionate and it's about to make itself real comfortable up your ass if you don't apologize to my buddy here right now."

Ponytail cleared his throat and mumbled "Whatever —sorry" as he walked off with his ponytail between his legs, so to speak.

"Yeah, that's right," Murphy called out after him. "My boy's wicked romantic!"

And then Murphy went back to the other end of the bar to drink beer.

"Wow. That was amazing," Donna said. "Here's my phone number. I want you to call me so we can arrange a time for you to come to my house and help me with a problem."

"Okay," Billy said. He was more than willing to help her, simply because she was red hot and he wanted to smash that. But he would soon learn that she was so much more than just a dump truck and nip nops.

And then they said goodbye to each other because Donna had to leave.

It was the month of Halloween, so when Billy saw Ponytail Guy sitting inside a nearby coffee shop when he left the Harvard bar with Murphy, he sauntered over and banged on the window. "Hey," he said to Ponytail when he got his attention. "Do you like candy apples?"

"I guess," said Ponytail, shrugging.

Billy slapped the napkin with Donna's phone number up against the window in Ponytail's face. "Well, she just gave me her numbah, so fuck you and your candy apples, mothahfucka!"

A few days later, after Billy got arrested for being too much fun, he called Donna and she gave him the address for the house her patient had left for her. She was having house troubles of all kinds—primarily the haunted kind. William was more than happy to help her with her pipe troubles. He laid her pipes good. Real good. So good that Donna never wanted another plumber. Even though they told other people and themselves that they were just friends, they did all kinds of things together. Billy did things to Donna's sensational body like no one else ever could. Donna kissed Billy all over and made him feel things he never felt with anyone else.

They did it in every room of that house of hers, in a lot of different ways. Ways that gave Billy the opportunity to show her how good he was with his tool. And his abs. And his butt.

They had so much fun together.

But one day, when they were fixing the house up, Donna said to Billy, "Billy, I want you to move in with me, but I need you to get rid of the ghost first, so we don't have to be scared."

"Don't say that to me," Billy said. "Don't say somethin' if you can't get a take back. You're gonna move into this house, and then you'll find out somethin' about me that you ain't gonna like. Like about how I like to jump off rooftops and break into Dunkin' late at night. I'm just some fling you're havin', meanwhile you'll go off and marry some guy who wears loafahs and doesn't got anywhere near as nice a butt as I do."

"First of all, your butt is fire—no one has as nice a butt as you do," Donna said, because she had not yet met any of Billy's relatives nor seen their behinds. "And second—what's a loafah?"

"You know—those boring shoes that boring guys who are born rich wear—loafahs."

"But I want us to be together, Billy. You and me, without the fears or the ghost. If you tell me you don't want to live with me in this house, then I will leave and you will never see me again. Even though you should be the one to leave because I am the one who owns the house. And even though we currently live next door to each other. But I need to go."

Billy gathered up all his stubborn, frightened strength and said to her, "I don't. But I will hunt the ghost for you so you can live here by yourself, because I am a good guy, okay?!"

Donna cried and left. She drove away from the house. Billy was now alone in the big house.

Well, not exactly alone...

As soon as Donna left, there was a thunderstorm. "Come out, come out, wherevah you are, ghost!" Billy shouted. "I'm not afraid a youse!" The lights inside the house flickered and then went out. But in the darkness, another flash of lightning revealed the ghost. "What do you want from me?!" Billy cried out.

The ghost just regarded him kindly.

"Who are you?!" Billy asked, loudly—for Billy said all things loudly.

"I am the Ghost of Parties Past," the ghost howled. The ghost was a gentle man with a beard and he wore a brown sweater and brown corduroy pants. He seemed very sad. But also scary, as it is very frightening to be confronted by a ghost, especially one who understands you as well as this one understood Billy, in ways that Billy was not yet comfortable talking about. Because even the most brilliant of geniuses are not fluent in the language of the heart until they realize it was the language they were born speaking— they just forgot how.

"Oh yeah? Cool, man, what's up, cocksucka?" He said that because cocksucka was sort of Billy's love language. It was rather charming the way he said it.

"What's up is I know about all your partying and shenanigans, Billy. I know about all the stuff you blew up. I know about all the penises you've drawn on the faces of people who were passed-out drunk. I know about the prank calls to the Afflecks and the time you lost your wallet and convinced the guy who sells hot dogs at Minuteman

Stadium that you're a time traveler and if he didn't give you five hot dogs and a beer the entire world would explode."

"Yeah, that was wicked genius of me. How'd you know? What—did you look at my file or somethin'?"

"There's no file, William. I'm a ghost. I just know things."

"Okay. Well, big deal—everyone knows about the partying and the shenanigans. I'm legendary."

"It's not your fault," the ghost cried out.

"I know."

"No, I mean it," the ghost said, taking one ghostly step closer. "It's not your fault."

"Whaddya talkin' about?"

"It's not your fault you're afraid you partied too much for too long and don't have what it takes to be a husband."

"Naw, naw, not you, man."

The ghost took another step closer, cornering Billy. There was thunder and another flash of lightning. "It's not your fault."

"Don't fuck with me, man. Not you too, man! Not you!"

"It's not your fault." The ghost whispered it this time as he attempted to embrace Billy, who was now weeping in a very manly, badass way. But alas, the ghost's arms just passed right through Billy. Because he was an apparition.

"I'm sorry," Billy sobbed. "I'm sorry I told Donna I didn't want to live with her, and I'm sorry you're dead."

Billy wiped away his own tears since the ghost couldn't do it for him. And then Billy said to the ghost, "And I am sorry that I must ask you to leave. So that I may in fact live here with the woman I love, Donna, after I drive away and find her and bring her back here."

"It's cool," the ghost said, smiling softly. "It's time for me to take a trip anyway. Gotta get back out there."

"Okay, mothahfucka," Billy said, also smiling softly. "You don't have to go home, but ya can't stay here. Me, I gotta go see about a girl."

And with that, the ghost nodded his approval and then vanished, along with the storm and all of Billy's fears of loving and being loved.

Then Billy drove away from the house, back to the apartment building he and Donna both lived in as neighbors, found Donna, they kissed, and then they drove back to the house again together. There, at that house, they once again did it in every room that night.

And they did it nastily, and happily, evah aftah.

billy

So this is happening.

I was listening to my favorite Meat Loaf song last night and wondering if there was anything I won't do for love, but it turns out I'll do everything Donna asks me to do.

Including participating in a fucking séance.

I cross myself when Donna isn't looking. Not in fear of ghosts or demons. In fear of my ma or Aunt Mamie finding out. If any of my older Catholic relatives hear about this I will be in so much trouble. But I'm doing it for Donna. And because part of me is thinking this is actually an elaborate role-play scene, like, taken to the next level. But if she's serious about it being a real séance, I don't want to ask. I'll just play along, like I always do. And I'll go to confession tomorrow to repent, just in case.

It is literally a dark and stormy night over here at the house. The night of a full moon, no less. It's not too cold though, which is good because Donna didn't think we should turn the heat on. She's brought a Costco-size bag of salt, a bunch of candles, and a Ouija board up to the master bedroom. Because this is where she feels the spirit's presence the strongest, she says. She has also brought a box of wine that her friend from work gave her. She calls it emergency trunk wine. Apparently trying to communicate with a spirit counts as an emergency. A pretty big one, judging by the number of glasses she's knocking back.

"Should you be drinking this much while Ouija boarding, Madam Belladonna?"

She polishes off the glass of wine and then smacks her lips. "I don't know how to do this without it. It'll be fine." She puts the glass down on a bedside table and claps her hands. "Wooo! Let's do this. Let the spirit communications begin!" She pulls a piece of white chalk from her bag. "Okay. I have to do a cleansing ritual and create a protective circle first. By drawing a pentacle on the ground. Or a pentagram? I need to draw a five-pointed star thingy."

Okay, this has to be RP. I roll up my sleeves. This is gonna be good. "You need any help with anything, Red?"

"No, I'm good. Piper texted me all the deets." She gets on her hands and knees on the floor and draws a big five-pointed star thingy. She's wearing a blouse, and I have a fantastic view of her cleavage. So far I have no complaints about this ritual. "Oh wait, can you turn off the light?"

I do. "Should I leave the door to the hallway open?"

"I think so?" She gets up and places four big white candles on the floor around the pentagram and then lights them. Then she lights a fifth candle, a tapered one, and holds on to it as she stands in the center of the pentagram. She waves the candle around. "I am clearing the air..." she chants, closing her eyes. "This is a safe space... I banish all negative entities... Only entities with good intentions may enter this space..." She opens her eyes. "Shit, I forgot the salt."

"I'll get it." I grab the twenty-five-pound bag of table salt and rip it open like it's one of Donna's tank tops. "What do I do?"

"Pour it in a big circle around the pentagram. Outside the candles. I think."

"You got it." I do that. It's not a perfect circle, but it's a full circle and there's still some leftover when I'm done. "Do I need to use all of it?"

"No, I think this is good," she says. "I hereby acknowledge that this circle of salt represents the boundary wherein all those who enter shall not be harmed." She closes her eyes again and hums something. I think it's the theme song from *Harry Potter*.

Then she opens her eyes, curtsies, and shrugs. "Okay, I think that's it. Now we bring that table and the chairs inside the circle and set up the Ouija board."

I carry a round table to the center of the chalk pentagram, and we each set a chair on either side of it. Donna places a brass candlestick near the edge of the table and puts the tapered candle in it. Then she unboxes the Ouija board and places it in the center of the table. I've seen these in movies and TV shows, of course. It's just a beige-and-black rectangle with the words *Yes* and *No* in the top corners, *Good Bye* along the bottom, the alphabet, a line of numbers, and a drawing of a sun and a moon. She places a plastic triangle thing on top of the board.

"This is the message indicator," she explains. "I will be the one communing with the spirit. It has to be only one of us so the spirit doesn't get confused. I will ask the questions, and we will patiently await the answers. Take a seat," she says. So serious, all of a sudden.

We take a seat in chairs opposite each other. "Do we hold hands?" I ask.

"No. We each place the fingertips of both our hands lightly upon the message indicator, which is otherwise known as a planchette." The detail she's going into for this scene is really chef's kiss. "Please do not purposefully manipulate the message indicator."

"Got it." I place my fingertips lightly upon the message indicator. "I shan't."

"Neither shall I," she says. Then she takes a really deep, shaky breath, exhaling through her mouth. "Okay. You ready?"

"So ready." Halfway to full mast ever since she lit the candles.

"Same. Okay. Here we go..." She closes her eyes. It is eerily quiet. The rain has stopped. The winds have cleared the sky of clouds. The full moon shines bright.

Donna clears her throat. "Good evening... We now invite friendly spirits to communicate with us... Is there a spirit here who wishes to communicate with us?" She opens one eye and glances down at the message indicator. We both wait. We hold our breath.

About ten seconds of nothing later, Donna sighs and says, "Is there a spirit here?"

A few more seconds of nothing.

And then something.

The dim light above the stairwell flickers.

The candlelight dances.

All of a sudden, I feel a cool breeze, the door to the bedroom slams shut, and all of the candles in the room go out.

Which is certainly not unheard of in a drafty old house at night.

But I can feel the hairs on the back of my neck standing up.

Because I'm cold.

The room is now lit by moonlight.

The message indicator moves to the word *Yes*.

"Holy shit," Donna whispers. "Did you do that?"

"No."

She shivers so hard I can hear it. "Okay...I'm gonna move it back to the center now." She doesn't say that she *didn't* move it. She slides the planchette away from the word *Yes*. "Hello. Thank you for joining us. Are you willing to communicate with us?" The planchette immediately slides back to the word *Yes*, like the spirit is impatient. "Okay. Thank you. Can you spell out your first name for us?"

After a few seconds, the message indicator slides to the *L*.

Then to the *A*.

Then to the *R*.

Then there's a long pause.

"Lars?" Donna asks. "Is it you?"

Then the message indicator slides jerkily to the *A* again.

"Lara? Are you Lara Olander? Lars's wife?"

The indicator slides to *Yes*.

Donna inhales sharply. "Okay. Hello, Lara. Do you know who I am?"

The indicator jerks away from *Yes* to *No*.

"My name is Donna. This is Billy. Is Lars with you, Lara?"

Hard *No*.

"Okay. We're here to help you, Lara. Is there something you need?"

Yes.

"Please tell us what you want."

The message indicator slides to *F*.

I.

N.

D.

"'Find'?" Donna says. "You want us to find something? What do you want us to find?"

Nothing.

No movement.

No sound.

And then all of a sudden—Donna's entire body tenses up. She leans back in the chair, almost like she's been shoved. Her head drops back. She trembles. If I didn't know better, I'd say she's already having an orgasm.

"Here we go..." I mutter.

Donna's eyes are shut. Slowly, her chin tilts back down and her eyelids snap open. Her gaze is blurry. She isn't looking *at* me so much as in front of me.

"Donna? You okay?"

She gasps. "It's you!"

"Hey. What's up?"

She looks around, stares down at her hands, places her hands on her tits, widens her eyes like she's never felt her own amazing tits before, and slides her hands down her waist to her hips and ass. "Oh, my heavens, my word, oh golly, oh gosh!" It's Donna's voice but also different. Younger. Naive. Still weirdly hot. "Oh, to feel my body again! After all this time! Or has it been no time at all?! Why, I can hardly remember time passing anymore and yet I still remember waiting an eternity for you to come back to me!"

"I know what you mean. That's kind of how it feels when I see you too."

Her eyes are so glassy. Like she's stoned. I guess it's from the trunk wine. "Oh, Lars. My love! Love of my life!"

Okay. Okay. This is weird, but I'm into it. "Hey, Lara. How ya been?"

Donna slaps my face. Not super hard, but it's a surprise and again—kinda hot. "How have I been? How have I been?! How dare you ask me that when I've been here waiting for you forever and ever?! You just left me all alone here!" She looks confused. She touches her lips. "Oh, but am I wrong? Were you only gone for a night? A day? An hour?"

She stands up, knocking her chair back. It falls to the floor. "Oh, Lars! You're here! That's what matters, isn't it? Oh, how foolish of me to be angry at you!" She reaches across the table and places her hands on either side of my face. Her hands are ice cold. "Oh, my

155

darling, my dear, please, please forgive me! Say you will, my darling, say you forgive me!"

"I forgive you."

"Oh, Lars! How I've longed for your touch!"

"I, too, have longed for your touch."

"I will cook for you, my dear husband, but first— but first!"

"Yeah?"

She pushes everything off the table. The Ouija board and planchette and candlestick go flying. She grabs my face and plants an urgent kiss on my lips. "Take me now, Lars! You must make love to me now, oh, please!"

She rips apart her blouse and lies back across the table.

"You got it." I stand up over her and start to undress. "Is this what you wanted me to find, baby? Your pussy?"

"My what?!" And then she puts her hand out to push me away. "Wait." She sits up. "Wait! We must find the letters."

"The letters?"

"Yes! Yes, now I remember! I've been looking for them everywhere. You must help me find the letters, you see?!"

"The letters *u* and *c*?"

"Nooooo! The letters you wrote to me, you fool! Where are they? Did you get rid of them?! I told you never to get rid of them! Why do you never listen to me?!" She screams and then covers her own ears, holds her head like she has a headache. A little melodramatic, but she's really into it. "What's happening? Oh no. I'm going away again."

"Just take a deep breath."

She wails and reaches out for me like she's being dragged away, and I grab her hand, but she drops back and lies on the table, staring up at the ceiling. Then Donna's eyes snap shut. She trembles and jitters and shakes. It's scary and weird and hot, and I have so many feelings about what's happening right now and I'm gonna have to tell my priest about all of them tomorrow.

Donna starts chanting, and it echoes all over the house. The hallway light flickers. The chandelier shakes. Donna's body jerks. The bedroom door opens on its own. Another door slams downstairs.

And then silence.

Donna lies on the table, totally limp, like after she's had a massive orgasm.

Which maybe she has?

Everything happened so fast, and I have no idea what's going on.

For a second it seems like she's not breathing.

"Donna?"

I touch her arm.

Her eyes open. She gasps. "Billy."

"Donna?"

"What am I doing on the table?" She slowly tries to get up, and I help her. "Why is my blouse ripped?" Her voice is hoarse.

"You don't remember?"

She touches her forehead. "Oh my God, how much did I drink? I feel so foggy." She looks around, then remembers I just said something. "Remember what? What happened?"

I help her off the table. "I mean, I already knew you were a good actress, but this was really something. You okay?"

She rubs her temples. "I think so?"

"Did you bring any water or just wine?" I look through her bag and find a bottle of water to give to her. "Drink this."

She gulps it down. "Oh my God. I've never been so thirsty."

"Yeah. Well. Lara was pretty thirsty too, lemme tell ya. Should we continue this on the bed, or...?"

"Lara..." She looks around and sees the Ouija board and planchette on the floor. "We have to close the session," she says. She hands me the empty water bottle, picks up the Ouija board and planchette, and places them back on the table. "Sit down and put your hands on the thingy again," she orders.

"Yes, ma'am."

With both our hands touching the thingy, Donna

says, "We now close this session. Thank you for communicating with us, Lara. Goodbye." Then she slides the planchette over to the words *Good Bye* on the board. She flicks my fingers away and places the planchette upside down on the table, away from the board. Then she flips the board over. "We now break the connection with the spirit world." She gets up to grab her purse and pulls out a sage wand, picks up one of the candles from the floor, lights it, and uses it to light the sage. Then she waves the wand around the circle and the room. "I clear the air, I clear the air, I clear the air... Okay, seriously, what happened? How do I not remember getting on the table?"

I can't tell if she's still acting or not, but I recount what happened. I tell her what she said. Or what Lara said. What she said as Lara. I tell her what Lara wanted. About the letters. And the making love.

"Wow. That's intense. I don't remember it. I mean, I remember contacting her and her moving the planchette... That *was* her, right? You didn't move it?"

"No. It wasn't me. But I mean, it was you, right?"

"No. It wasn't me either."

"*Oh-kaaayyy.*"

Donna disappears into her thoughts for a few minutes, and I let her.

I move the table and chairs back to the corner and use the broom and dustpan she had brought up to clean up the salt.

"I can't believe I forgot about the letters," Donna finally says.

"What letters?"

"Before Lars died, he gave me a box full of letters he'd written to his wife. He said he wanted me to have them. He told me never to destroy them. But I didn't read them because I could tell they were personal. So I put them in my closet because it made me sad. I guess I should bring them to the house."

"Wait, so there *are* letters? You're saying this as you? As Donna?"

"What? Yeah. It's me. Lars gave me a box of letters he'd written to his wife."

"Okay..." It doesn't feel like we're gonna fuck anymore...

She sighs. "Well. Thanks for doing this with me. This was interesting."

"'Course," I say. "It was definitely interesting."

She smiles. "I couldn't have done it without you."

"I wouldn't have let you do it without me." I lean against the broom, and we just stare at each other smiling for a few magical seconds.

Finally she breaks the spell. "I think I need some fresh air. Come outside with me for a bit?"

"'Course." She could have asked me if I'd go to Mongolia with her for a bit and I would have said of course.

I help her put on her coat before we leave the

room. It's so cold in this house. The lights don't flicker as we walk down the stairs. It was probably just weather related. It's fine outside now. We stand on the front porch, both of us with our hands shoved into our coat pockets, looking up at the full moon. The sky's clear all around it, and it's so bright. There's a light breeze rustling the trees, but other than that it's incredibly quiet.

Donna laughs quietly. "I didn't want to be here after dark, and I come here with a Ouija board on the night of a full moon." She shakes her head. "I really do appreciate you doing this with me."

"It's really no problem. You know how to keep things interesting."

That really makes her laugh, and her laugh echoes around the property. "Well, I guess we better get on with the date training, huh? Get out and do something normal next? What's an activity you enjoy that you'd want to share with a girl you're dating?"

I stroke my chin, pretending to think about this, as if I haven't been thinking about it for days. "Well, I mean. I enjoy an awful lot of activities, Red. I am a very well-rounded fellow."

"Oh yeah?"

"Oh yeah. But there *is* something..."

billy

"Dee's havin' an MVP-type season. Of course, he's the heart of the team," my dad is explaining over an ancient hibachi grill, holding a Sam Adams in one hand and pushing sausages around with a spatula in the other.

"But so is Dash. And the team plays mean. Like he does," my friend Murphy is explaining to my father. A beer in one hand for him and a sausage dog in the other.

"A defensive end like Dash isn't gonna win MVP. Even if he has thirty sacks. And a running back hasn't won it in years. So you're both wrong," my other friend, Titus, says.

"Mark, whadda you think?" my dad asks my brother.

My brother takes a considered sip of his idiotic cup

of sparkling apple cider. "I'm just happy to be out of the house. My wife is the real MVP."

I roll my eyes at that even though he can't see me. Guy sucks up to his wife even when she isn't around. What's that about?

"She comin' with my grandkids?"

"Yeah, they're already up in the box with Ma."

Me and my pops, brother, and friends are doing what we've done for the last couple of decades. We're tailgating in the Minuteman Stadium parking lot. We don't have to anymore. I have a luxury box with full catering. But tradition is tradition. Especially when it comes to the Tommies.

"Billy, what are you so quiet ovah there for?"

"Sorry, Pops," I say, like I've done something wrong by not running my mouth.

"He's thinking about his special guest!" Murph says in a singsong voice. Murph is demonstrating the exact kind of behavior I was worried about when I invited Donna to this game.

"Hey, you be cool and you be nice—all right? All of you. Or I'll get you kicked out of the friggin' stadium, and you know I can."

"Whoa, chill, bro. We'll be nice to your girlfriend," Titus says. He sounds very disappointed, which I do not like.

"She's not my girlfriend. She's a very important...neighbor."

Now, you may think this is where Murph, Titus, my brother, and my dad would ask why I would invite a female neighbor to a Tomcats game. Even an important neighbor. And maybe question why this neighbor is so important and why I'm acting all nervous while I'm waiting for her to show up.

Except they're men. So they ask no follow-up questions and return to debating the MVP and the successful season the Tommies are having so far.

"Hey, guys." I turn to find Donna approaching and giving a nervous little wave. She's looking adorable, with her Philly Lightning cap, hair in pigtails, filling out a Lightning jersey in a way that team does not deserve to have their jersey filled out. I never thought in a million years I'd enjoy seeing someone in that jersey, but there it is.

"Oh, hey. Everyone, this is Donna. Get your *boos* out now and get it over with." The boys boo Donna and her Phillies jersey good-naturedly. Donna curtsies in her jersey, and my heart does a little flip. Damn, she's cute.

The men all shake her hand and introduce themselves to her.

Then they return to the hibachi, but there's a hush now, like they don't know what to do with themselves. It's not like women aren't around sometimes during tailgates. Maybe no one quite as smoking hot as Donna. But maybe it's the fact that there's an enemy in our camp now and they don't know what to say to her if they have to be nice.

Awkward silence was not the start I was hoping for.

I'm about to punch through this ice, but Donna is the first to speak up.

"Do you mind if I have one of these?" Donna points to one of the cans of Sam Adams.

"Knock yourself out," Murph says, vaguely glancing at her face. I can tell he's trying really hard not to acknowledge the lightning bolt on her hat or her shirt.

Donna smiles. "Thanks." She takes out her keys, punctures the can, turns it on its side, cracks the tab open, and shotguns it.

I laugh, and the boys immediately take notice.

I don't know who starts the chant, but soon every single guy, including me, is chanting, "Go! Go! Go!" We're still Tommies, and she's still a Lighter, but for one glorious shotgunning of a beer, we are all one.

Donna empties the can with a satisfied sigh, crushes it, and throws the can into a nearby barrel. We all clap, and the boys give her high fives. I couldn't be prouder. The energy is much more relaxed now, and the conversation returns to its normal shouting.

"Where's your mom?" Donna asks.

"Oh, she's already up in our seats."

"Up, huh? Nosebleeds?"

I grin. "In a manner of speaking."

I tell the guys we're gonna bounce and bring her up to our seats. The look on Donna's face as she takes in the private luxury box is pretty satisfying. We've got comfortable seats, an amazing spread of food and drinks, a huge, big-screen TV in the corner, and of course, a wide, direct view of the field.

"Billy...how can you afford this?"

I shrug. "I know a guy." Of course, the guy I'm talking about now is the ticket guy for the Tomcats who took a whole pile of my money in exchange for the box. But she doesn't need to know that. "Hey, I have another surprise for you."

I point to the corner of the box where her oma and opa are sitting. Her oma and opa are dressed in full Philly Lightning gear, head to toe. I wasn't expecting people who grew up in Germany to have adopted the Philly teams so wholeheartedly. I thought maybe they were just trying to support their granddaughter. But when the first words out of her opa's mouth wasn't *Hello* or even *Guten Tag* but "The Tomcats *schtink*!" I knew they were true-blue fans.

"What?! Oma? Opa? What are you doing here?" Donna's voice is joyful, and it makes me so happy.

"Your kind *und* energetic gentleman friend Wilhelm flew us here," her opa says.

"Surprise!" her oma says as they both get up to hug Donna. "Ooof. *Püppchen*, you need to eat more.

Have a strudel. I brought some with me on the plane."

Donna turns to stare at me, shaking her head. "Billy, how...?"

I shrug again, saying, "I know a guy." Of course, this was the ticket guy at the airport who took a whole pile of my money in exchange for two tickets on a last-minute flight.

This is why I like having money. Being able to gather my friends and family together and give them an experience like this. And Donna. And her family. The whole *knowing a guy* thing used to be totally true. I got what I got through guile and charm. I've been able to do the things I do because I meet people at crazy parties, remember their names, and I save phone numbers. Donna doesn't know I have a fuckton of money because I don't broadcast it. I lease a Volvo. I still live in the same apartment building. But also because, as a rule, we didn't get to know each other personally until recently.

But now I do want her to know me. The real me. And I don't feel like the money is me. It's just something that I have. But the guy I know who really makes things happen—that's always been me.

"And who might this lovely young red-haired lady be? Billy, why haven't you introduced me?" I get a loving smack up the backside of my head.

Here we go.

"Oh, hey, Ma." I throw my arm around Ma and squeeze. "This here is Red, otherwise known as Donna Fischer."

"What a pleasure to meet you, Donna Fischer. You are simply stunning and adorable with those pigtails, despite that god-awful hat and shirt!"

"Thank you, Mrs. Boston. I mean, O'Sullivan." Just when I think Donna couldn't get prettier, she blushes pink as a peach.

"So I guess this means Nolan lost the bet, huh?" Ma says, elbowing me. "What do we win?"

"Nothin', Ma. It's not like that."

Ma puts her fists on her hips. Uh-oh. That is not a good sign. "Whaddya mean nothin', young man?"

"Hey, Donna, why don't you check on the spread. The drinks, everything's all included. Go to town."

"What are you doin' tellin' your date to check on the spread? What kind of animal did I raise? Go get her an appetizah, for cryin' out loud."

Donna, seeing that I need a save, helps me out. "I do prefer to peruse the catering table myself. Pleasure meeting you, Mrs. O'Sullivan."

"You too, hon—such an absolute pleasure!" Ma says pleasantly to Donna as she leaves to check out the game-day buffet. Her smile drops, along with her tone, when she turns back to me. "Explain to me, William, who that full-figured young redhead is, whose grandparents you flew in from Philly, if she's not your girlfriend."

"She's my neighbor."

"Neighbor, huh? Is that like how they changed the word *girlfriend* to *partner*? Is neighbor the new shawty? Is she your boo thang?"

"What? No. She lives in the apartment next door to me. Not my girlfriend or my partner. She's teaching me how to date properly."

"I'm sorry—what's this?" My ma holds her hand up to cup her ear while leaning in and scrunching up her face. "She's teaching you how to date, you say? But not actually dating you?"

"Yeah. She offered to help."

"And why didn't you come to *me* for advice? Huh? What am I, chopped livah? I don't know how to date? I got your fathah to propose after two dates. Two."

"What? Why would I ask you about something like this? You're my mothah."

This is how most of my conversations with my mother go. She never knows if I'm being serious, and I never know what she's going on about. We love the hell out of each other; we just don't speak the same language like me and my dad do.

"Exactly—because I'm your mothah! You're supposed to come to me for everythin'."

"Well, I didn't come to you for this."

"Well, you're crazy to pass on my advice for anythin'. One day my heart'll give out and you'll be sorry. I love ya more than anyone in the whole friggin' universe will evah love ya, but you're outta your damn mind."

"Right back at ya, Ma."

Meanwhile, I overhear my pops talking to Donna's grandpa.

"I don't know, Mister Opa." I don't think my dad gets that *opa* means grandfather. "The Lightning do have a good offense, but I think the Tommies can run on them and their defense is next level." But my father is using his peacetime, *give the other team a little credit* voice. He doesn't mean any of it. He thinks that every time the Tommies lose a game, it was a glitch in the matrix or the refs were paid off. I do appreciate the effort.

"You forget one thing, Herr O'Sullivan," Donna's oma chimes in.

"And what's that, Missus Oma?" my dad says with a kind smile.

Donna's grandma holds up a dainty finger to emphasize her point. "The Tomcats *schtink*."

Christ Almighty.

Maybe this was a bad idea.

Maybe it would be better if the Lightning were way up. Then my family would just drink and eat and lose interest in the game. Except my dad. Or maybe it would be better if the Tomcats were crushing them, so my family would be even more generous to our misguided guests who chose an enormous loser to cheer for. But it's tied at halftime. The tension is high in the box, so my friends go roaming around the stadium to stretch their legs.

"Do you want to go with them?" Donna asks.

"No," I answer honestly. I take a seat next to her in the back row of the luxury box. "I'd rather sit here. This is where a guy would sit if he was on a date, right? Next to his girl. Not that I'm saying you're my girl, but in this hypothetical educational scenario that is for my own edification, you are the girl. The woman. The female date."

I say a lot of things in my head. *Good one, hotshot! Keep going! You're a fucking stud!* But never, not once in my entire life, have I ever told myself to stop talking. But I'm telling my mouth to shut itself now. My mouth, having no experience with this, keeps on moving.

"But if the lesson is ovah, I guess we can just watch the game."

"No, class is still in session, Mr. Boston."

"Oh yeah? How'm I doin'?"

She looks around. My father is continuing his MVP

argument from the parking lot with Donna's opa, even allowing Opa to throw in a Philly player or two. Her oma is discussing "young people nowadays" with my ma while bouncing my niece and nephew on their laps.

"I'd say you're doing pretty great, Mouth. The whole *flying the grandparents out* thing? Baller move. How did you do it?"

"Their phone number is on your fridge." I shrug. "I took liberties. It's what I do."

She laughs. "It sure is, Mouth." She sighs. "I needed this."

I furrow my brow. "What do you mean?"

She shakes her head while staring out onto the field. "I haven't been able to sleep very well since the séance."

"Yeah. Right. That was intense. Hot, but intense."

"You thought it was hot?" Donna looks slightly horrified.

"I meant cool. It was cool." Donna's face is telling me that is not the right word either. "I mean it had drip. Or rizz. Or whatever the kids are sayin' nowadays. Anyway, we probably shouldn't talk about it around my ma. Whether it was real or not. As a God-fearing Catholic she would excommunicate us. Lovingly, but completely."

"Got it," she says. "But you do understand it was real, right?"

Before I can respond to that, we're interrupted by a lady's voice. "Knock, knock. Mind if we come in?" Hannah Decker, owner of the Boston Tomcats, is standing at the doorway, flanked by members of her staff.

"It's your joint—you can go wherevah you want."

"Hello, Mr. Boston," she says in the *we meet again* tone of an archenemy.

"Hello, Mrs. Decker." She approaches us, and I get up to shake her hand. "Nice to see you. Give my best to your husband."

"Please stop trolling him on X."

"I'm pretty sure he loves it. This is Donna Fischer, my...neighbor."

"Neighbor? So that's what people are calling it nowadays. Pleasure to meet you, Ms. Fischer."

"Likewise. Congrats on the season so far. I hear you have a winning record, even though your team stinks." She cups her mouth and chants, "Lightning! Lightning!"

"Ahh, a Phillies fan. Yes, we're five and one. You'd think that would get people to cut me some slack on social media..." Hannah raises a brow at me. I have indeed been critical of her moves in the past, especially one that concerned our former star quarterback who is now her husband.

"Hey, don't look at me—I'm comin' around. Dash has been an absolute beast."

"He has indeed. I hope I'm not bothering you, but I figured we could chat about our involvement with your venture."

"Uh, yeah, of course. Donna, would you excuse us?"

"Of course. Pleasure meeting you, Ms. Decker."

"Likewise."

I pull Hannah aside. I can explain away a lot of stuff. Access to a luxury box. Access to an unlimited supply of costumes and props. Access to all the time in the world to play with her and fix up her house. But explaining why I would have business with an NFL franchise would be tough to pin on "knowing a guy."

We talk about a sponsorship deal and having some of Hannah's players at the Make-A-Wish event next month. This lady might think I'm a buffoon for trolling her and her husband, but she knows a good business move when she sees one.

We shake on it. "Sounds good. My people will be in touch with your people."

Hannah turns to leave, then takes a step back and leans in, lowering her voice. "You know, Mr. Boston, since you're always offering me unsolicited advice on social media, why don't I offer you some too."

"Go on."

"Don't wait to secure a deal. You have something good, someone that would make a strong team, then make it happen. Because if they're a free agent, it's incredibly easy to lose them to someone else."

I nod. "I hear you."

"Enjoy the second half, Mr. Boston."

"Likewise. Go Tommies!"

"Go Tommies!" Mrs. Decker punches the air and exits with her staff.

I sit back down next to Donna.

"Hey," Donna says. "What was she talking about? You're doing business with them?"

"Oh, yeah, you know. Sports business and whatnot."

She seems to buy that, but she's looking at me funny. Like I'm a cute puppy or something.

The second half of the game starts. "You can head back down with your friends if you want," she says to me.

"Nah. I'm where I want to be." I look at Donna. Really look at her. And she looks at me. We aren't pretending to be other people. We aren't wearing costumes or pulling faces or covering how we feel. For a moment we're just two people who have—whatever it is we have—between us.

I clear my throat. "So how am I doing, really? Decent date?"

"Yeah, it's really good so far. So, if I *were* your girl..." She gives a little shrug. "What would you do next?"

"Well, if you were my girl, you wouldn't be wearing that godforsaken jersey."

"Oh yeah?"

I nod, a cocky smirk on my face. "Yeah. You'd be wearing mine."

Donna looks like she's considering this real hard. She removes her jersey and tosses it onto the chair next to her. I take off mine and hand it to her, and she puts it on. We're both wearing T-shirts underneath. We've taken our clothes off in front of each other in private so many times, but this feels different. There are other people around, family, but this feels way more intimate somehow.

"How do I look?" she asks, getting up and twirling around so I can see. It's a custom jersey that my dad got me a long time ago that says *O'Sullivan* on the back. And it damn well just about takes my breath away to see Donna wearing my name.

"Stunning."

She sits back down next to me and leans in. "That's good. That's real good, Billy. Girls like to hear things like that. So what else would you do?"

"Well, if you were mine, and since you're wearing my jersey and my name, I'd lift up your chin here, like this." I place my fingers under her chin.

"Mm-hmm." Donna murmurs. "And then?" Her voice is breathy, her eyelids getting heavy.

"Then I'd kiss you. Like no one else was here. Like

we were the only people in the world, even though we're surrounded by family."

And I lean in and do just that. I kiss her. And I don't care if my family sees. I don't care if her family sees. I don't know what kind of explaining I'll have to do later to justify kissing someone like this who is just "my neighbor."

Because I'm done justifying not kissing her like this to myself. I need my lips on hers more than anything. More than I need my team to win or air to breathe.

As I'm kissing her, a great cheer erupts around us. We smile into our kisses, both of us thinking the same thing. That they're cheering for us. But it turns out the Tomcats have scored a touchdown. The old Billy, the Billy of even a month ago, would be sad he missed it, wanting to high-five with his friends down by the railing.

But I'm not missing anything.

I feel right in the middle of the action.

Right where I want to be.

donna

BILLY BOSTON AND THE SCARLET SPITFIRE

"But why is Wilhelm not your boyfriend, *Püppchen*? Why do you not want happiness with a man? Wilhelm is not Trevor. Only Trevor is Trevor."

It's been a long day, and I don't have it in me to argue with this woman. Also, *I'm* starting to wonder what my problem is. "I know he's not Trevor, and I am happy, and Billy is great, but—"

"His team *schtinks*," Opa interjects. "But Wilhelm is great."

"Exactly. But this is just a no-strings thing that we have, Oma." I don't know how to explain to her that I'm starting to think I want more of Billy and with Billy and from Billy, but I can't bring that up with *Billy* or I might end up with no more Billy.

"What is this no *schtrings*? Why should you not have all of his *schtrings*?" Oma asks.

"We just hang out and fool around and have fun without the commitment. It's really great!"

My oma snorts. "*Mädchen. Püppchen.* Between a man and a woman this is not a thing."

"Ach! *Schtop* pestering her! Everything has its time, yah? You know the saying, Donna, *Alles hat seine Zeit.* Let our girl have no *schtrings* until she wants *schtrings*, Helga."

"Thank you, Opa."

"But you need to nail that man down soon, *Püppchen*, before someone else will. He wants *schtrings* with you, but he will not wait forever, I think." Opa sounds like Sigmund Freud all of a sudden.

"Yah. 'Everything has its time...'" I can literally hear my oma rolling her eyes at him.

"Okay, well, I'm almost at the house, so I need to hang up now. Love you guys. Glad you got home safe."

"Say hello to Wilhelm for us!" Oma says before I hang up on her.

Billy is already at the house. His car is parked outside, and it's alarming how happy I am to see it there. He has his own key now. We don't have keys to each other's apartments, but he has a key to my haunted house. That's something, I guess.

I'm still wearing scrubs because I just got off work, but I comb my fingers through my hair and apply lip gloss in the rearview mirror. I've got the wooden box filled with letters that Lars gave to me for safekeeping. Hopefully we can just read them aloud to Lara, she'll find peace and have closure, and then she'll be on her merry way and I can focus on the cranberries and my sunroom and my shiplap. Hopefully.

If she doesn't leave, well, I probably won't be able to sell a haunted house, and I can't live here, so I'll just keep living in the city and paying the property taxes on this place because my late patient, who was so very sweet, forgot to leave me money to pay for taxes and upkeep and, oh right, he also didn't mention his wife's ghost.

So this has to work.

Not that I'm in a big hurry to move out of the apartment, because that would mean moving away from Billy. The thought of it makes the rims of my eyes sting and the tip of my nose tingle. Even though I work twelve-hour shifts, even though Billy's always out doing God knows what, God knows where most of the time, I've gotten used to living under the same roof as him. But if he does start dating someone seriously, it will be a lot easier for me if I don't have to hear him come home with her, so I really do need a ghost-free house to move into.

As I step up onto the front porch, I get a better grip on the wooden box and start to flip through all the keys on my key ring to find the one for this house. But before I do, the front door pops open. I wait for Billy to appear, but he doesn't. Stepping through, I find the inner door open as well. I guess he forgot to shut them.

He isn't waiting to greet me in the front hall either. I find Billy's toolbox on the first step of the stairwell, but I do not find Billy. "Hello?"

No reply.

I don't hear any movement downstairs.

And then I hear humming from upstairs.

Shit.

Not the upstairs humming again.

"Billy?"

No reply.

I clutch the box to my chest and pick up a flathead screwdriver from the toolbox before going upstairs. I do not plan to stab a ghost with a screwdriver, and I also don't think I'll do much damage if there's an axe murderer up there. But if there's another dove stuck in the closet and I have to pry open the window, this will definitely help.

But now I hear more than humming.

I hear singing.

And the hint of an echo that can only mean one thing—Billy is singing in the bathroom. It's not that damn Chumbawamba song. It's not a Meat Loaf song. Nor is it a Neil Diamond song.

I don't recognize it, but it sounds like a classic.

"Every morning, every evening

Ain't we got fun?
Not much money, oh, but honey
Ain't we got fun?"

I pause when I reach the door of the en suite bathroom. It barely sounds like Billy. He's got that old-timey ragtime vibe going. It's weird.

Very weird.

As I'm about to step into the bathroom, I get a flash of an image of Jack Nicholson in *The Shining* when he's in a shower with that woman.

If Billy is showering with the ghost of Lara Olander in my house and singing to her, I will murder him and then I will make his ghost live here with me forever.

But he doesn't appear to be in the shower with anyone else, living or paranormal. He's in the tub, stepping back and forth, holding his caulk gun in both hands and then twirling it like it's a cane, while he's back to humming. Is that the Charleston? Or a foxtrot? He's really into it, so I just stand here watching him for a bit. And he doesn't seem to realize I'm here at all, even though I don't see an earbud in his ear.

I clear my throat.

He still doesn't acknowledge me.

"Billy!"

He sees me out of the corner of his eye and shouts, "Mothahfuck!"

I scream.

We both freeze and stare at each other for a few seconds until we can really focus on one another, and we burst out laughing.

"Jesus," he says. "I didn't hear you come in." He steps out of the bathtub and runs his fingers through his dark hair. He looks so cute in his unbuttoned flannel shirt.

"Yeah, well, I heard *you*..." I almost lean in to kiss him. Which is not a thing that we do. But it feels like it should be. "Got your caulk out, I see."

"Awww yeah. I've been putting this caulk to work all over this house."

"What was that song you were singing?"

"Huh? When?"

"Just now."

"Was I singing?" He looks genuinely confused.

"And dancing a little bit."

"I was?" His brow furrows. I don't know if I've ever seen Billy look confused like this before. He usually just goes with the flow. "That is so weird. I've had this song in my head ever since I got here today. But I don't think I ever heard it before. And I definitely didn't realize I was singing it."

Yeah, that checks out, and that's not creepy at all...

"Well...sounded like you were having fun!"

"Whatcha got there?" He nods at the box of letters. "Cigars?"

That makes me laugh. "No! It's the letters."

"What letters?"

"The ones Lara wanted."

His face is blank.

"Remember, you said that she told you she was looking for the letters Lars wrote to her?"

He looks less confused now. "Ohhhh. Yeah, right. From the Ouija night."

"Yeah."

"So we're doin' that again?" He sounds oddly excited about the prospect of contacting a ghost again.

"Yeah. I left the board here and that bag of salt is still in the bedroom, so I guess we should contact her that way. I could just try reading the letters out loud to see if that does it for her, but I don't really feel her presence right now—do you?"

"You mean Lara?"

"Yeah."

"No, not yet. I mean, you're not acting like her right now, right?"

"What?" Now I'm confused. "When was I acting like her?"

He finally puts his caulk gun down on the counter and rubs his forehead. "You know. When you got up on the table and said that stuff."

I frown at him. "I wasn't acting like her. I was..." I get a chill just thinking about it. "I was possessed by her, I guess."

He smiles and shakes his head at me like I'm

messing with him. But surely he can see from my face that I'm not. "Wait. You swear to me that you weren't acting last time? You weren't pretending to be possessed?"

"I swear! What—did you think that was role-play or something?" I guffaw.

He rubs his lips together. "Huh? Noooo. I just thought you were messin' with me."

"Oh my God. You thought I did all that for a scene? That I went to Costco to buy a twenty-five-pound bag of salt just to spice things up?"

"Donna, we could put on a Broadway show with all the costumes we've collected over the past couple of years. What's a bag of salt? All that matters is I thought you were into it and I was really into it too."

I laugh so hard I snort. "Oh my God! You are such a guy!" I can't even remember the last time I laughed this hard.

Except that now I'm starting to question what actually happened with that Ouija session. Maybe I did make the message indicator move? Not on purpose, but maybe subconsciously? Maybe I'm just clinging so hard to an old story about getting my heart broken that I'm refusing to move forward and made up a ghost to hold me back? Is Trevor the metaphorical ghost I'm haunted by? I don't remember lying down on the table at all. It's like I blacked out for a while. Maybe I was drunker than I thought I was. Maybe I'm so used to role-playing with Billy that I just slipped into RP mode...and unconsciousness. Surely that's the preferable explanation.

That's better than owning a haunted house.

I guess?

I can't stop laughing. This is ridiculous. My goal in life for the past couple of years has been to keep things as uncomplicated as possible outside of work, and now the guy I have role-play sex with is helping me renovate a house that might be haunted, I'm starting to have feelings for him because I'm coaching him on how to date someone else, and I bought a Ouija board because a teenager told me to.

Maybe this is exactly what I need.

I look at Billy's perplexed face again, and my heart aches a little because one day I might not be able to look at that face at all.

But I'll worry about that later.

"Well," I say, wiping away the tear of laughter from one eye, "let's get this over with."

"Okay," he says, washing his hands in the bathroom sink. The water is, thankfully, no longer cranberry red. "I gotta let that caulk dry anyway."

He helps me set up again. It's not nighttime yet, so it's a lot less creepy. Though, I am one hundred percent less tipsy, so now it kind of feels like one more thing to cross off the to-do list for fixing up this house. Kind of. There's slightly less of a chance I'll be possessed by a ghost when I'm painting the living room walls.

After I've drawn the pentagram and done the space-clearing ritual, Billy and I sit opposite each other at the round table. I place the box of letters in front of him, to the side of the Ouija board.

"I think you should read the letters. Okay? Once we've contacted her. *If* we contact her. Are you good with that?"

He nods. Not exactly apprehensively, but with much less enthusiasm than he usually agrees to things.

"Thank you. I haven't read them yet, like I said, because I knew they were personal. I have no idea what they say. And there's a chance I might get possessed again. But whatever happens, just keep reading the letters until you've read her all of them. Okay? There are ten in there. They aren't very long. But I don't think she'll move on until she's heard all of them."

"What if she takes over your body again and she wants my body?"

"I mean. Resist it."

He makes a face like I asked him to walk to the moon.

"Have you never said no to a woman who wanted you to make love to them, Wilhelm?" I tease.

"I've never said no to a woman who looks like you,

Red," he says softly. "I don't think I can look into your face and resist you if she tries to kiss me."

Dammit, Mouth. "Well...that's really sweet. But she's Lars's wife, so..."

He sighs. "Okay, so let's do this. I'm gonna read some letters out loud. Right on."

"Yeah."

"Should I read them like Lars?"

"You don't have to. I mean. If you can. Like Lars when he was in his twenties? He didn't have a strong Boston accent like yours. At least not when I knew him. He traveled a lot."

"Oh, okay. So don't sound as unbelievably sexy as I usually do. Got it. Good note."

"He actually talked kind of like an old-timey movie hero. Just read it like an actor from a black-and-white movie, if you can do that."

"I shall do my very best," he says, combing his hair down with his fingers so it lays flatter on his head. It's usually all wavy and kind of unruly. And he's clean-shaven. Billy looks so different all of a sudden. I'm realizing he has the same coloring as Lars did when he was younger. He had a few black-and-white photos of himself with Lara around his condo, but I didn't spend much time looking at them.

We place our fingers on the planchette. I tell myself *not* to manipulate it, as if that will do anything. Clearing my throat, I say, "Good afternoon... We invite

Lara to communicate with us... Lara Olander...are you here?"

I barely get the chance to inhale before the room temperature drops and the planchette moves to *Yes*.

"Okay. Hello again. I've brought the letters from Lars."

The planchette moves jerkily to *R-E-A-D*.

"Yes. We're going to read the letters to you."

Billy looks up at me, and I nod at him to go ahead.

He opens up the wooden box and takes out the stack of letters, in their envelopes. "Okay, we'll just start with this one, I guess." He unfolds a piece of note paper. "'My darling,'" Billy reads, without the Boston accent. "'My scarlet spitfire.'" His eyebrows raise, and he makes a guttural sound of approval.

I roll my eyes.

"'My Lara, it has been twenty-seven hours since we said our goodbyes at the train station in Virginia. I am back in my home state, but it no longer feels like my home without you here. I have written you five other letters. Three of them were unreadable because I was so frantic to get the words out. Two of them were inappropriate, but very honest ramblings of what I long to do with you. I have been pacing about my flat, thinking of you. Your scent, which still lingers on my fingers and my coat. Your flaming-red hair and alabaster skin. The way your blue eyes dance with deviousness and desire when you smile at me. The way your lips taunt me with flirtatious words and kisses. That mouth, that mouth... Your mouth will be the death of me, my sweet devil woman.

I am losing my mind here without you. This is the cruelest separation I have ever known. I must return to you, Lara. You are too far away. I can no longer conceive of a life without you in it. Come to me, or I shall come to you. How can we be together? Lara, Lara, Lara. There is only one other four-letter word that means so many different things to me, and it also makes me think of you and what I want to do to you.

I cannot believe your parents refuse to get a telephone.

Write me back immediately.

I demand a response.

I'll be thinking of you, always, as I go about my business here. I will not come to you until I get word, tormentor of my mind and heart and soul and flesh. Do not torment me for sport. Your claws are in me, but I will not play this game forever.

Yours, yours, yours,

Lars.'"

Well, shit.

I can see why Lara was missing those words.

I had forgotten that my fingers are still on the planchette until it slides across the board to the *M*. To the *O*. To the *R*. And to the *E*.

"More," I say to Billy.

"Comin' right up," he says, as if he's mixing drinks at that bar. He reads another short letter, one that obviously came after that first one he read, chronologically. She obviously wrote him back, he went back to see her, and her mouth did another number on him. But she sounds very sweet too. She was probably just young and only knew how to tease men.

As soon as Billy's done reading, the planchette spells out *MORE* again.

Billy unfolds another letter. "'My darling Lara, my love is building a house for you. It sounds like a line from a poem, but it is simply the truth of what I am doing. For you. For us. If you will have me now and forever, dear Lara, we will live together in this house. We will harvest cranberries and have chickens and goats. We will fill this house with children and love. Please, Lara. Come to me in Middleborough. Let me take care of you. I have rented a small old house in town, and we can live there until this new house is complete. I will come to Virginia again to ask your father for your hand next week if I hear from you. Please. I need to hear from you soon. Your devoted lover, admirer of your mind, and slave to your delightful moods, Lars.'"

Well. I don't think Lara is *making* me swoon. She doesn't have to. Lars wrote some damn fine love letters. And Billy is doing a damn fine job of reading them. A little too damn fine. I'm starting to get a little lightheaded. Or heavy headed? My head feels light and it's like my blood feels all fizzy or something, but the air feels heavy all around me.

Did I forget to eat today?

Probably.

Billy starts to read another letter. "'My love, my soul, my scarlet spitfire. The way you gave yourself to me this time. I am over the moon. I miss your smile and your voice, but you'll be here soon. All I hear is your voice in my head. Your voice and our song.'"

I watch him, but my vision is getting blurred. Darkening around the edges, like filmstrip when it burns. I can hear Billy's voice but also someone else's whispered voice. Flashes of memories that feel like dreams because they aren't mine.

Such a bewildering swirl of emotions. So many lines are blurred, and I can't parse out what's coming from Lara and what's mine. Frustration and impatience and the exhilaration of having a body again and love. So much love.

I feel my hands on my chest, over my heart, and then I watch as my hands reach out for Billy.

It's like I'm watching a movie of myself from the inside.

I don't feel like I have control of myself anymore. *She* does. Almost like I have invisible strings controlling me. Like she's the puppeteer and I'm a marionette.

But the face I see before me isn't Billy's. It's a young Lars.

"Lars!" I stand up and grab his face. "Lars! My love, my life!"

"How ya doin'?" Billy says.

Part of me knows it's Billy's voice, but it sort of splits off into someone else's. Lars's voice.

"Oh, my love, our song! Yes, our song!" I start singing.

"Every morning, every evening
Ain't we got fun?"

Billy stands up and sings.

"Not much money, oh, but honey
Ain't we got fun?"

My feet move around the table to Billy, but I'm not the one who's moving them.

"The rent's unpaid, dear
We haven't a bus."

Billy puts a hand on my waist and takes my hand in the other.

"But smiles were made dear

For people like us."

We dance and sing. I don't know this song, but I'm singing it. Billy is too. Together, we sing:

"*In the winter in the summer*
Don't we have fun
Times are bum and getting bummer
Still we have fun."

"Oh, my love!" I cry out. I feel giddy. Or she does. Lara is having the time of her afterlife. "Oh, Lars! You're back, you're back, you've come back to me!" I kiss him, all over his face. "Oh my darling, I'm all yours! Take me here and now! Take it out for me—oh, how I've missed it so!"

"Uh-oh." Billy lets go and steps away from me. "Nah, I gotta finish readin' these letters now. Sit back down there, you." He points to the chair. "I command you to sit back down and listen."

"Oh, but we're together again at last, you silly goose! We must never let each other go!" I hurl myself at him. Or rather, Lara hurls myself at him.

And then my lips press against his.

My memory of kissing Billy like this at the football game gets overtaken by a memory that isn't mine—of kissing Lars.

The unabashed rush of love is so beautiful it brings tears to our eyes—*my* eyes.

"Oh, my love, my love, my love! Don't ever stop kissing me!" It's not quite my voice, but it somehow matches my feelings.

He looks at me. Looks into my eyes, trying to figure out who's saying that to him.

"Lars. Lars!" *I wanted to say* Billy, *dammit!* "More, please, don't stop! Oh, my darling, Lars!"

He looks disappointed, grips my arms and pulls away. "Lara," he says, authoritatively. "Sit down in that chair so I can finish reading my letters to you. You need to hear them. Then we can really be together."

"Why, yes sir," I purr. Both of us are having a distinct reaction to that tone. My body returns to the chair and listens to the rest of the letters.

Apparently Lara got cold feet and was nervous about leaving her parents and her life in Virginia. Lars had promised his mother that he wouldn't leave Massachusetts again now that he was home from the war. The fear and sadness is overwhelming. I can't stop the tears. They're pouring down my face. I know how much they love each other and I know how it all turns out, and it's all just sad. Even Billy is getting a tremor in his voice.

He gets to the final letter in the box and has to clear his throat before reading it.

"'My love. My scarlet spitfire. My bride. The month I spent without seeing you or hearing from you brought the kind of agony that I never want to experience again. The loss of you was the loss of everything. Opening the door to this house and finding you standing there on the porch, your beautiful face wet from the rain and your tears, was the great surprise of a lifetime. Greater, even, than our chance meeting when I was visiting a friend. You came to me. You pledged yourself to me. And you married me. Not in haste, but in pure joy. Now I must wait for you to return with the rest of your belongings. We'll have a wedding here one day, my love, I promise. This house is ready for us and all the love we have to fill it with.

Our life together will begin.

There is so much I could say to you, my darling. Fortunately I have the rest of my life to tell you. Just know that anything I ever tell you means this: I love you.'"

He looks up from the letter and directly at me.

"I love you," he says again. "I love you." And there's no trace of the black-and-white actor or Lars. It's pure Billy Boston baritone.

"Oh, I love you too!" I cry out. But it's not Lara's voice. It's mine. I get up and reach across the table to grab his face and kiss him. It's not the invisible puppet strings that are making me do it.

And then I get dizzy, so dizzy.

The room is spinning.

I don't feel Lara anymore—she's gone.

It's just me kissing Billy.

We finally break the kiss.

I still feel a head rush, but I don't think it has anything to do with Lara leaving.

I have to sit down again because my knees feel weak, and again, I don't think it has anything to do with being possessed by Lara.

Some voice in the back of my mind reminds me to close the session.

I place my fingers on the planchette. Billy takes a seat and does the same. We slide it to the words *Good Bye* on the board.

And now it's done.

Lara got what she wanted.

She heard what she needed to hear.

I'm just not sure who said *I love you* to whom just now.

I just know that it felt so good to say it.

I think the ghosts are gone.

But now I feel haunted by what we just said.

billy

IT'S THE WICKED GREAT PUMPKIN ALE, BILLY BOSTON

Manhattan: *Hey, Boston. Come meet us for lunch. We're going to Harvard Yard Sale for apps over in Worcester-boroham. Then we're gonna hit up Manwich for some brisket over in Lagerdale. I know a guy who owns an ale house called Party for Your Gullet down by Foxenchester by the Sea. You in?*

Manhattan: *PS it made my thumbs itch just typing those words.*

Fucking Nolan: *Come join us for lunch, fuckface.*

I stare at my phone. This text chain is totally normal. For us. No *Hey we're in town*. No explanation on how they were able to get away from their families to visit Boston. Just *Come meet us*. Only usually I'm the one who does the inviting. And implicit in a simple lunch invitation is the promise of absolute fucking debauchery.

What is not normal is my reaction.

I'm not sure I want to go. Because going would mean I'd have to exit my apartment. And if I time that wrong, I might run into Donna. And if I run into Donna, we might have to unpack what happened at her house the other day, and I don't want to scare her.

Because as I was reading Lars's words in what I imagine might have been Lars's voice, they didn't feel like just his words to Lara. They felt like my words to Donna.

To paraphrase Robert Downey Jr. in one of the greatest films of all time—*Tropic Thunder*—I know who I am! I'm the dude playing a dude, disguised as another dude who's reading a letter to a dudette who's possessed by another dudette, and they're pretending to be in love with each other!

Except I think it might be the opposite of that. I think Donna and I might be pretending *not* to be in love with each other. At least I know that's what I'm pretending. And I want to believe that she feels the same way—about only pretending to not be in love with me, I mean. But if I'm wrong, I ruin everything and it's all over.

Knock, knock, knock.

I put my phone away. Maybe it's her? Maybe she's

being braver than I'm willing to be. I suck it up and open the door.

"Hiya, fuckhead." Instead of Donna, I find Nolan staring at me, with his evil blue eyes.

"Too busy to respond to texts from your favorite cousins?" Declan asks.

"I was getting to it. Why are you so impatient that you showed up at my home?"

They share a look. A look I don't trust.

"We're husbands and fathers now. We're just excited to go out."

"Yeah, that's all it is," Nolan adds, completely unconvincingly.

I narrow my eyes. "What else?"

They look at each other again, then back at me. "What do you mean 'what else'?" Nolan, that Irish demon, asks, all innocent-like.

"I know you're husbands and fathers now. Softer. Fat and happy from marriage. However. You may leave the game, but the game never leaves you. I know you hear glasses clink on a warm, dark night and think about our epic nights of debauchery. The Blue Moon calling to you like a werewolf."

"I don't drink Blue Moon, ya gobshite."

"I was being poetic, fuckface. The point is you are caged animals who've been recently released. Tired and broken down dads that you are, you're coursing with adrenaline. If you wanted the kind of night you know only I can provide, I'd already be kidnapped and have half a bottle of Jack Daniels poured down my throat by now."

They look at each other again. Then back at me.

"Piper told us there was a girl, and our wives told us we have to help you with her," Declan says.

And there it is.

"And how, pray tell, do you plan to help me with her?"

"We just want to meet her," Nolan says. But he doesn't say it like a concerned family member. He says it like an Irish gangster.

"No," I say simply.

"Whaddya mean, no?" Nolan says.

"I said no."

I see Nolan gearing up for a fight. The man doesn't have a lot of experience hearing no. I don't have a lot of experience saying it, so we're both in uncharted territory.

Declan holds up a hand to stop Nolan. "Wait. Why don't you want us to meet her?"

I open my mouth. Close. Open it. Close it again. The opening feels right. The closing, like me saying no, feels brand new to me.

How can I explain that I don't want them to meet her because it suddenly feels very complicated with Donna?

"She's at work," I say. "Probably," I add quickly.

"Well, let's just see." A real casual *fuck you* shrug from Nolan. "No big deal." He saunters over to Donna's apartment.

"How do you know that's her apartment?"

"Piper told me she lives next door—it's either this one or the other."

Nolan's feckin' Irish luck led him to pick right on the first try. I step out into the hallway but am then completely frozen in place as he knocks on her door. She opens it.

"Oh, hello," Donna says in surprise.

"Hello, lass. My name is Nolan." He offers his hand, and she shakes it tentatively. It's then she notices me and Declan standing in the hall. "I'm this *eejit*'s far more handsome and intelligent cousin. And this tall pint of Guinness in an oxford shirt is our cousin Declan."

Declan walks over and offers his hand. "Nice to meet you."

"Very nice to meet you," Donna says. Her voice sounds confident, but her eyes keep checking in with mine.

"We were wondering if you would like to join us for some libations. Our dear young relative, Piper, has had the pleasure and simply raved, and we would like the same opportunity. Drinks are on us, of course."

Donna looks at me through my cousins. We're both considering a million conversations we should have had that now we can't. "That sounds amazing. Let me get my purse."

Nolan calmly chalks his pool cue as he finishes his story. "So Billy wakes up somewhere dark. He's hearing loud music, the stompin' of feet. He reaches up and opens the lid of whatever he was in."

"What were you sleeping in?" Donna asks me.

I squint one eye, trying to remember. "Some sort of weaved chest or basket thing?"

Donna turns her rapt attention back to Nolan, who continues the story. "So he pops out, and he's on a stage with dozens of Indian wedding guests doing a choreographed dance to a Bollywood song."

"Oh my God. What happened?"

"Well, this is where Dec, Eddie, and I found him. We were at the entrance to the ballroom, and the whole wedding party kind of stopped and stared at him. And without missing a beat—right *on* beat, in fact—Billy starts doing the "Night Fever" dance from *Saturday Night Fever* he learned in high school gym class. The DJ quickly changed the music, and they all just sort of went along with it."

"I can't imagine. I mean, I can actually." Donna laughs and grins at me.

I give her a wink. "I just happened to be wearing a gold chain and a sick three-piece bell-bottom suit..." I say with a shrug and then take a pull of my beer. "But they taught me the Bollywood dance after that."

Donna laughs her beautiful, full laugh. But I know what she's thinking. She's thinking she wants to see me do that dance in that suit, and she will one day get her wish. This has been more fun than it had any right to be. I don't know what I was worried about. Donna's not interested in making things heavy or dramatic. It's one of the many things that makes her so amazing.

"If you'll excuse me, boys, I have to go to the bathroom," Donna says. "Don't touch your balls while I'm gone." She points at the pool table, and we all laugh.

"She's really fun," Declan says.

"And gorgeous," Nolan says.

"Yeah, she's amazing," I say.

"So why is she not your girlfriend?" Declan asks like a reasonable human being.

I sigh. If I can't be honest with her, I can at least be honest with them. I tell them about our arrangement. That it's a no-strings thing and it's just fun. I leave the role-play stuff out. But I tell them that she's also been teaching me about dating like a normal human being.

I cast a furtive glance at the bathroom doors, making sure Donna is still in there. "And I'm getting a little confused. I mean, I like her. But I like her because it's fun. But if we make it serious, I'll ruin it for both of us."

"I don't think you're confused at all. It sounds like you more than like her, Billy. I mean, you're a millionaire and you're still living in the same apartment you had before you had all that money. Why? Because she lives next door. And it's not just the sex. You're *dating* her."

"She's *teaching* me how to date."

"Yes. By dating you," Nolan says, plainly. And then he adds, "Ya fuckin' moron."

Of course, that's it, isn't it? We haven't been role-playing as people dating. We've been role-playing as people who are pretending not to date while actually dating. Like I've been role-playing as a guy who's not in love with Donna. When in reality, I've completely fallen for her.

And then I say something that I am one thousand percent sure I have never said before in my entire life —certainly not to these guys: "I don't know what to do."

"You tell her how you feel," Declan says, like it's the simplest thing in the world.

"But what if she doesn't feel the same way and I ruin it?"

"I say we stop playing footsie with getting drunk and get absolutely hammered. She needs to see the real Billy Boston."

I look suspiciously at Nolan. There's been something about him all evening that I couldn't quite put my finger on. "You've been pushing us to go hard since we got here. Why is that?"

"Billy boy, this is what we do. We get wasted and go on adventures. It's why we're here."

I finally put it together. "Wait a minute. You're hoping she'll see how crazy I can get and run!"

"What? Is that true?" Declan asks Nolan. At least Dec is good enough not to be in on it.

Nolan gets a dark look on his face. He's fun, but even Fun Nolan can be fucking terrifying. "Billy's half right. I didn't come all this way for a couple of pints and a nice chat. I love bein' a dad more than anythin', but I came to pay tribute to the old Nolan. The one where *I* was the one who needed to be put down for a nap. Where *I* put things into my mouth I shouldn't. Where *I* made the mess instead of cleaning it up. But yeah, if she so happens to be put off by that and Billy doesn't have a date for Granny's birthday shindig, then that would be a double win in my book."

"You piece of shit. You'd fuck up my chance at happiness to win a bet?!"

"If showing her your true form ruins the relationship, there was no happiness to be had, boyo."

I turn to Declan, who has his palms up facing me, claiming innocence. He has to talk sense into this degenerate.

"While I'm not a fan of his motives"—Declan side-eyes Nolan before turning back to me—"he's right. You need to be honest about what you want. And you need to be honest about who you are. And I didn't secure all this childcare and come all this way for a couple of beers. Nolan's right. I live for Maddie and Ciara. They own my soul. And it's exhausting. It's problematic. And wonderful. But this wolf needs to hunt."

"That's the spirit!" Nolan pats Declan on the back.

Donna returns. Her smile drops as I see her clock the strange energy she just entered into.

"What's wrong?" she asks.

"Nothing," I say quickly.

But the Irish devil speaks up. "We were just discussing what the rest of this evening might look like. A nice calm, pleasant, boring, average, run-of-the-mill evening like we're having. Or a Billy Boston Special. A tale you can half remember and believe even less."

"I've already had a lot to drink. I thought this *was* you guys going out?" Donna says.

There's a lot of scoffing and laughing. *You poor, innocent thing.* "Oh, no. This is nothing," Declan says, his jaw set. I can see in his eyes that this domesticated cat is ready to go feral again.

"You've never seen Billy's true form. I suppose you've only met William O'Sullivan. You've never seen the true face of Billy Boston," Nolan says, like I'm the Loch Ness monster or the friggin' Babadook.

Donna looks up at me. Her eyes are deep and open like there's something important she wants to ask me. Instead she says in a soft, serious tone, "I'd like to see that."

I look nervously at the guys and then back at her. "I don't know. It can get pretty crazy."

Donna shrugs. "I'm up for crazy. We're good at crazy. Right?"

My face is hard with indecision. I'm not sure I want crazy with Donna anymore. Not *just* crazy or fun anyway. I want real. But Declan, and even fucking Nolan, are right. If she doesn't know all of me, then it can never be real.

"Okay," I say in defeat. This was too good to last anyway. I rub Donna's back, thinking silently, *It was nice knowing you.*

"Shots!" Nolan calls out into the night in the same exact tone that a general would yell *Charge!*

And that word usually ends up being the last one I remember of the night.

FOURTEEN

donna

AMERICAN HANGOVER STORY

Oh God.

Where am I?

Oh no.

It's the house.

Am I on the bed?

How did I get here?

I can't move.

Everything hurts.

Or wait.

I don't feel anything.

I feel dead.

Am I dead?

Am *I* the ghost?

Did I lick a hairbrush?

It feels like I have lava in my belly. Wait. It's in my

throat. I'm gonna vomit. Wait. No, I'm not. Yes, I am! ...No.

Wait. I'm a nurse. Am I? I am. Check vital signs. Without moving body. Or thinking too loudly. Or blinking. Or breathing too much...

Slowly, slowly, my index and middle fingers move to the opposite wrist, and I find a pulse. I can confirm that I am physically alive. Now I have to count...one, two, three, four, yeah, I'm hungover.

What happened?

...

Billy.

Billy Mothafuckin' Cocksucka Boston happened.

My brain is smiling, but my face is trying to go back to sleep. Where is that maniac? And how is it possible to be this hungover and so horny at the same time?

"Afternoon, sunshine!"

"Shhhhhhh!"

"Oh, sorry," he says, but I swear his voice is exactly as loud. "How do you feel?"

He leans over me, and I grab his shirt to pull him down for a kiss. Ten seconds ago, my tongue was so dry I could have used it to sand the back porch rails, but even though I'm barely conscious I am salivating for this man all of a sudden. There's no telling if the elevated heart rate, body temperature, and blood pressure are hangover related or Billy related, but I know for sure that the hangover is a direct result of hanging out with this guy.

"Horrible," I say when our lips finally part. I'm smiling now, I think. Maybe not with my face, but with my fatigued, dehydrated soul. "Just awful."

"Sorry to hear that, Red." He stands up, and I have to close my eyes again because looking up at him is bad. "I had groceries and hangover food delivered. What strikes your fancy, milady?" I can hear him moving around and taking things out of paper bags. "I got all the bottled water you can drink. Ginger ale. Gatorade. Coconut water. Saltine crackers. Greasy fast-food burgers, because I have personally found that this helps best with hangovers. You need protein and fat to digest the sugar from the alcohol."

"That is not how alcohol metabolism works."

"Trust me. It is. I also got Tylenol, Advil, Tums, Alka Seltzer, Pepto Bismol, Bloody Mary ingredients, mimosa ingredients, Guinness... I got coffee, tea..."

"You drank even more than I did. How are you not hungover?"

"Oh, I am, but y'know. I get knocked down, I get up again. It takes a lot to really knock me down, though."

"Oh my God." I try to laugh, but it comes out like a yawn and then a groan. "Ow. You're a maniac."

"You're kind of a maniac yourself, Red. You really kept up with us. We were all impressed."

I snort. "Please. I believe it was the three of you who had to keep up with me." I don't actually remember what they had to keep up with, but it feels like the right thing to say. I try to arch an eyebrow with my eyes closed, but I don't think my face is moving. "Did my eyebrow go up?"

"Nope. Did you want it to?"

"Yeah. Where are your cousins? Are they okay?"

"Yeah, those cocksuckas made it home just fine."

"They're back in New York already?"

"Yeah, we dropped 'em off at the airport before we came here, remember?"

"No."

"Maddie and Cora both sent me pictures of them sleeping in their respective bathtubs."

"Aw, that's nice."

"So, you, uh..." He massages my thigh. "You weren't spooked?"

"By what?" I hear buzzing in my head. Or near it.

"By me."

I snort. "Why would I be spooked?"

"Well, some people find the full Billy Boston experience a little extreme."

"You were magnificent." I reach for him. With the tip of an index finger. There's that buzzing again. "Do you hear that? The buzzing? Why is it so loud?"

"It's your phone. You want it?"

I sigh. "I don't want to open my eyes. Can you check to see who it is?"

I feel him reach under my pillow. "It's your friend from last night. Chelsea."

"From last night?"

"Yeah, she's textin' to make sure you got home okay. And she thinks I'm hot. And she sent you a bunch of pictures and a video."

"Huh?"

I squint my eyes to watch the video that's playing on my phone. It's of me and Billy on a small stage, singing "Monster Mash" into microphones. The camera pulls back to reveal Declan dancing and Nolan playing the keyboard. Declan appears to be taking his shirt off. And then it pans around to show one or two hundred people in Halloween costumes singing and dancing along with us. Then there's a close-up of Harley Quinn, who says, in Chelsea's voice, "That's my bestie, bitches!" right before the video ends.

I get strobe light flashes of memories of being in a motor boat and climbing up onto the side of a yacht. "Did we crash a Halloween party cruise?"

"Well, that depends on your definition of crashing a party," Billy says. "Is it crashing a party if your friend tells us where she is and we decide to join her even though we don't have tickets and then we make that mediocre party awesome? I think not."

I text my friend a thumbs-up emoji and close my

eyes again. "I've never done anything like that before," I tell him.

"Well, if you hadn't been there that guy might have died."

"What? What guy?"

"After we did the Time Warp that guy started choking on an eyeball grape and you Heimliched him."

"What's an eyeball grape?"

"You know. Grapes that are decorated like eyeballs."

I save the pictures Chelsea sent me to my photo library and scroll through some other pictures. I bring the phone closer to my face, blink, and look closer. "That is a fantastic Steven Tyler costume," I marvel. I am such a huge Aerosmith fan. "That is great makeup. It looks just like him."

"That's not a costume," Billy says matter-of-factly. "That's Steven Tyler. You don't remember being at his estate?"

"What? Doesn't he live in Marshfield? How did we get there?"

"I know a guy with a helicopter."

I scrunch up my face, hoping that will help squeeze memories out of my brain cells, but I got nothing. "Oh, wait. Did I cry on his couch?"

"For a little while. But it was a happy cry. You told him about how you lost your virginity to 'Dream On.'"

"Ohhh noooo. I carved penises into all of his jack-o'-lanterns."

"Yes, but in your defense, he didn't say you couldn't."

I try to cover my face with my hands but end up smacking myself. "Ow."

"You okay?"

"I don't know."

"Tell me what you need."

I smile again. With my face. I think. "Mouth," I say.

"Mine?"

I think about nodding, but then I remember that I never want to move my head. Ever. "Yeah."

"You got it, Red." He places his mouth on my mouth again. And then he parts my lips with the tip of his tongue and kisses me slowly and deeply, exactly the way I want and need to be kissed. The weight of his body presses me into the mattress and nothing hurts anymore. I no longer feel like a corpse, I feel languid and sultry. Except there's that growing pressure between my legs. A gently throbbing ache. I want to engulf him with my vulva. But in my sleep, without moving or taking my clothes off.

"I am so fucking glad you're still with me," he whispers when he pauses for air. Then he kisses my cheek and my jaw and my neck.

I open my eyes. My vision is blurry, but his handsome, stubbly face comes into focus. His wavy brown hair and beautiful brown eyes. "Hey. Somebody drew a *W* on your forehead. For *William*?"

"That's not a *W*." He grins and gently kisses my forehead. "That's a butt. You said it was a portrait of *my* butt, in fact."

"Oh. Your butt's much nicer than that."

"Thank you." He kisses down my neck again, fondling and kissing my breasts over my shirt.

"Why wouldn't I be with you?" I ask, shutting my eyes again because I have a clearer picture of him when my eyes are closed. My fingers find his hair, the back of his neck.

He's breathing so heavily now. "Donna," he exhales. "I know you don't feel good, but I wanna fuck you so bad right now. It'll be real fast but also real slow, I promise. I'll barely take your clothes off and you don't have to move—you can go back to sleep if you want. I just think I'll die if I can't be inside you."

"Yes. I want that. Yes."

"Oh, thank God."

"Billy?"

"Yeah?"

My mouth started moving before my brain could catch up, but I think I know what I want to say. Before I can second-guess myself, I just say it. "I haven't been with anyone else since we started doing this..." I am too tired to brace myself for his response.

"Yeah? Me neither, baby. It's just you now."

Oh, thank Christ. "Good. Put it in me."

"Fuckin' A. I will." He carefully tugs at my sweatpants.

Sweatpants? I'm wearing sweatpants. They feel like big sweatpants. I definitely was not wearing these when I left my apartment. "Whose pants am I wearing?"

"I really don't know," he says as he continues to pull them and my panties down to my thighs. "When we were giving those tourists that late-night Freedom Trail tour you kept complaining that your jeans were too tight, and next thing I know you were wearing these sweatpants under your Continental army coat and you said you needed to go to an ATM because you gave Nelson your last five pounds."

I have no memory of that.

And I don't care because Billy's hot, hard cock is already pressing inside of me and I didn't have to open my eyes or move, just like I wanted.

He moans, and it's so sexy. It's too loud, but it's so sexy how relieved he is just being inside me. "This okay?" he asks as he barely moves his hips. It's so, so sexy.

"Very. Mouth," I demand.

He kisses me, and I wrap my arms around him while he fucks me in slow motion. Or I guess this is what they call making love. It's so good. My blood is pumping again, to the rhythm of his thrusts, and I'm coming alive. Billy is slowly fucking me back to life, and I didn't have to ask him.

This is the part of being in a relationship that I'd forgotten about. Being in bed with someone, two warm bodies joining together with no big discussion, no fanfare. It feels like a dream. I don't know what time it is, I don't even know what day it is, I just know that last night was thrilling chaos and this is the sexiest kind of peace I've ever experienced. I never felt this connected to Trevor, ever.

"Why does this feel so fucking good?" he groans quietly. "I gotta move more. Okay?"

"Yes." I rock my hips and squeeze my thighs together.

"I'm gonna come, baby," he whispers.

"Come inside me, Billy. Don't pull out. Okay?" I want to say *I love you*. I want to say so many things, and I'd like to think it's just the hangover that's preventing me from saying them.

Heat radiates through my body from my belly, and I have a deep, slow, expansive orgasm. Different from anything I've had before, but it happens right along with Billy's shudder and heavy sighs. Time stands still, or maybe I fall asleep for a minute, or maybe this really was a dream.

"That was fucking awesome," he says, kissing me as he slowly pulls out of me.

My eyes flutter open, and the way he's looking at me, I think he felt it too. That deep, intense connection. That need to say *I love you.*

He opens his mouth to say something, pauses, then combs his fingers through his hair and says, "I'm gonna go clean up—hang on."

He's only gone for a minute, I think, but cold air caresses the skin on my bare thighs where he once was. When he comes back, he uses a damp towel to wipe between my legs, which feels even more intimate than what we just did. I love him. I open my mouth to say it.

But Billy says, "That was like we're teenagers and your parents are in the next room so we had to be real quiet."

Oh.

"That was hot, right?"

Oh.

"We never did that one before, huh?"

"Nope."

"You okay?"

I am now, I think to myself. *Thanks to you. I almost gave you my heart. And that would have been a terrible mistake. This is why you're so good for me, Billy. Not because you're fun and lovely and kind and generous and sexy and make me feel alive in a way I've never felt before. Not because I could imagine giving you my heart for the rest of your life and taking care of yours for the rest of mine. No.*

You're good for me because you remind me why I can't. Why we just pretend. We make our scenes as ephemeral as life itself. Because it all ends. I lie here feeling like death, in the house of a woman who took care of a man's heart, my patient's, until the end of her days. But her days ended too soon, and with no one to care for his heart, it shattered. She didn't mean for it to. That's just life.

Thank you, Billy.

"Yup" is what I say out loud.

He twists open a bottle of water, chugs it, then sits on the bed next to me and brings it to my lips. "Can you lift your head to take a sip?"

I nod, raise my head a bit, and drink a little water.

"You good?"

I nod. A lie.

He gets up and looks out the window. "Gettin' dark already. I'm gonna turn on the light in here, okay?"

"Sure."

He switches on the chandelier and the light bulbs flicker. They won't stop flickering. "Oh no," I groan. "The lights."

"What about 'em?"

"They're flickering again."

"They aren't flickerin'."

I squeeze my eyes shut and then reopen them. He's right. They aren't flickering. I just need electrolytes, I guess. "Oh." I pull up my pants—or Nelson's pants, I suppose—and slowly, very slowly, sit up. "I'm gonna take a shower."

"Oh yeah? You ever taken a shower here before?"

"No. But you ran the shower after the caulk dried, right?"

"Yeah. It seemed fine. I still think we need to get a home inspector over here, though."

"I'll take my chances," I grunt out as I hoist myself off the bed and onto my feet.

"You want company?" he asks.

"No. I will take an Advil, though."

I close the door to the bathroom and turn on the tap in the bathtub, adjusting the temperature of the water before pulling the lever for the shower. The water pressure is impressive for an old house. I brush my teeth and check my reflection in the mirror above the sink. I look exactly as good as I feel, which is not very good. No wonder Billy doesn't want to spend the rest of his life with me.

Yeesh.

These are hangover thoughts.

I just need to wake up.

I let my clothes fall to the floor and step into the tub. The water is clear and hot and even though it feels like a hundred pinpricks against my skin, this is exactly what I need to get my brain and body out of this funk. The shower curtain billows, like air has been let into the room.

"Billy?"

No answer.

I peer around the curtain, but I see no one in here. The bathroom is slowly filling up with steam because there's no ventilation. Billy's right about bringing in a home inspector. If I end up selling this place I'll have to anyway.

There's no shampoo or soap either, so I just rinse off, giving myself a blast of cold water before turning off the faucets. I slide open the shower curtain, feeling a rush of icy cold air as I reach for a towel on the towel rack. The lights flicker off and on again, and I'm sure I didn't imagine that.

Or maybe I'm not so sure of anything anymore.

Drying off my face and body, I grab another towel for my hair. Wrap my hair up in it. That was probably a bad idea, getting my hair wet, I am realizing, because I didn't bring a hair dryer. I have no recollection of how we got here, but I'm guessing we Ubered. Or *cabubered*? Why is that word in my head? I'm not ready to spend the night, so we'll have to leave soon. Although I can't assume that Billy's going back to the apartment too, because apparently I can't assume anything with him.

I go over to the counter, where I left a comb. The air is still steamy. I pull the hand towel from the wall hook, and just as I'm about to wipe the mirror, I watch in horror as an invisible finger writes the words *TELL HIM* in the steam on the surface of the mirror.

I freeze.

I open my mouth to scream, but nothing comes out.

"Billy..."

The bathroom door flings open, and a chill runs down my spine, but Billy doesn't walk into the room.

"Billy?!"

Still not there.

I look back at the mirror, and I see the reflection of a red-haired woman behind me—not me—it's Lara. I spin around, but she isn't there. I scream. "What do you want from me?!" I cry out. "We read you the letters! What else do you want?!"

"Donna?!" Billy comes running in.

I keep screaming.

"What?! What happened?"

"She's here! She's here!"

"Who is?"

I bury my face in his chest. "Lara! She was right behind me!"

"Donna, there's no one else here."

"Look what she wrote on the mirror!"

"Where?"

"In the steam! On the mirror! I watched her write it!"

"Donna..."

I do not like his tone.

"Donna, there's nothing written on the mirror. Look."

I turn to look. The steam has cleared. In the room and on the mirror. Which of course it did, because the door was open. "It said *Tell him.*"

He shakes his head, grinning. "Babe. You're just seeing things again."

Boiling hot blood heats my face and my ears. "Oh, of course I am. I've just been imagining everything, haven't I?"

"You're just hungover, that's all."

"But it said *Tell him*—I saw it!"

"I'm sure you think you saw it," he says, so loudly I am sure he has awoken my ancestors in Germany.

"Don't yell at me."

"I was very much not yelling just now, which is my point exactly. You're hungover, so all is not what it seems."

Yeah. Exactly.

And then I hear a knock. Or a thud. Another knocking thud. Like someone's banging against the walls from inside the walls. I suppose I'm imagining that too, but I look over at Billy, and his eyes widen. It's so loud. Metallic clanging now. Everywhere. And I know it's not my imagination that it sounds *angry* and Billy hears it too, and he's scared.

"We gotta get out of here," he says. "Put your clothes on."

"What do you want?!" I cry out.

"It's just the pipes," he says. "I'm gonna hire a contractor, and we are not coming back here until everything's fixed."

I cover my ears and close my eyes. I am so tired. "Why is this still happening?"

I can hear Billy's muffled, loud voice telling me to get dressed.

I do. He helps me get dressed again. I hear him tell me he's getting an Uber.

The lights are flickering. All of the lights. "The lights?" I ask.

"Yeah," he says. "There's a water pressure issue, probably. There might be a leak somewhere, affecting the wires. We gotta go."

"My hair is wet" is all I can say.

"Keep the towel on!"

He tosses me my bag and my coat, takes my hand, and leads me downstairs.

I stop on the landing, let go of his hand, and say, "I have to use the Ouija board! I have to ask her what she wants me to tell him!"

"Are you out of your fucking mind—we are leaving this house right now!" he yells, and before I can run away from him he's lifted me up into his arms and he's carrying me downstairs and out the front door.

"What do you want me to tell him?!" I yell out to the house.

"Donna. Stop yellin'. There's no ghost. It's just you and me, all right?"

I guffaw at that. "Yeah. Sure. Just you and me and my colonial parents sleeping in the other room!"

"What?!"

"It was never just you and me, Billy! It was always us pretending to be someone else!"

His jaw clenches. His nostrils flare. I would find it hot if he weren't such an insufferable man who refuses to see what I see and to feel what I feel and to know what I'm thinking without me having to explain it to him. "Let's not say anything we'll regret while we're hungover, Donna."

Thank God I didn't tell him I love him while he was ejaculating inside of me. He could never love me the way Lars loved Lara. "Great idea," I say. "Let's not say anything at all."

He sighs and shakes his head. "That's not what I meant."

"Ohhhh, poor little misunderstood Billy."

He wrinkles his brow at me. "Okay. Let's *not* say anything."

There's a flash of headlights up ahead as the Uber turns onto the private road that leads to the house.

I slide into the back seat, lean into the side door, and put my bag in between us so there's no chance our legs will touch during the ride back to the apartment. I huff and cross my arms across my chest, glaring out the window. I can feel Billy watching me from his side of the back seat. I close my eyes. All I see is the message in the mirror.

Tell him.

Tell him what?

What does she want me to tell Lars?

"Donna."

The look on her face... I saw her—I saw her in the mirror.

"Donna, we're home."

I open my eyes.

We're parked in the street in front of our apartment building.

I guess I fell asleep.

The towel is still wrapped around my head. We say nothing as we go inside and take the elevator up to the fourth floor. I rifle through my bag, trying to find my keys, with no luck.

"Lemme help," he says, like he's an exasperated dad and I'm his bratty kid.

I'm too tired to argue with him.

He pulls my key ring out of my bag immediately, like a magician.

"Thanks."

"You want me to unlock the door for you?"

"Sure."

He does. Then he opens the door and hands me my keys.

I start to go inside.

"So, you want me to give out candy with you tomorrow, or...?"

Pausing, I say, petulantly, "Don't you have a big Halloween party to go to?"

"Usually, but I don't have to go to that. I mean, unless you wanna go with me?"

"No, I'm definitely not up for it." He's just being polite. Or he just wants me to go with him to give him tips on how to pick up other women. "But...you should definitely go."

"Oh." He looks surprised and disappointed.

It almost makes me shut up. But I don't. "I mean, it's almost November. When's your grandma's birthday party? You need to win that bet. Right? You need a real girlfriend."

He stares at me, blinks once. "Right. I do."

I reach out to punch his arm. "Congratulations— you're ready to date for real. I hereby pronounce you a graduate of the Donna Fischer Dating School. You get an A-plus, kid." I try not to let my voice crack too much by adding, "Whoever ends up being your girlfriend is going to be a really lucky lady." I pat his arm because I don't seem to want to stop touching him.

"Right." His voice has gone so cold.

I shiver.

"'Kay," he says. "Well, happy Halloween if I don't see you tomorrow, then."

"Happy Halloween," I say.

And then I close the door.

billy

BILLY BOSTON AND THE SOURCE OF HIS STONES

"What's with the Harry Potter costume? Didn't you wear that, like, a decade ago?" Murph asks as we enter the party.

I am, indeed, dressed as sexy Harry Potter. The costume is not cut in some weird way to make it sexy, it's just a normal black robe, black-rimmed glasses, and wand. I just can't stop how sexy I am while wearing it. But Murph is right—this is a really old costume. I couldn't completely remove the butt Donna drew on my forehead, so I'm saying it's a lightning-bolt scar.

Of course the true reason I'm wearing a decade-old costume is that I couldn't really care less about this party.

"It's retro," I say in a half-hearted attempt to defend it.

"Well, you look like you're Harry Potter from the unreleased book *Harry Potter and the Saddest Sack of Shit*."

Oh, is my face doing what my soul is feeling? Whoops.

The music kicks into another gear, and I don't feel a need to respond. The party is at an abandoned building in the Fort Point district.

Just as a wine expert—or sommelier, if you're fancy—can smell and swish and taste all kinds of notes in a single mouthful of wine, I'm like that with parties. I don't need to experience the entire evening to know what's up. A few seconds of sampling the vibe and I know the vintage of a soiree.

I'm a soiree-lier, if you will, and my expert opinion is that this is going to be a great fucking night. The vibe, the energy, the lighting, the costumes, the exact note of the drone of people talking all around me. All of that tells me it is going to be one of those epic nights. Like Las Vegas 2012 or Tampa Bay 2019. Halloween de Boston '24 could be a very fine vintage indeed.

And I could give a fuck.

It ain't what I want. But this is what I need. I need to get back to being Billy. Billy is fun. He's a party. He's not a guy you date. And certainly not a guy you marry.

I'm a little shell-shocked by what happened with Donna. I've never felt closer to another person.

Coming inside her after our epic night together felt right. It felt like coming home.

I keep going over it in my head. Turning it into a role-play—was that not the right thing to do? I did it for her. I thought she'd feel what I was feeling and get scared. I didn't want her to run away.

Instead she pushed *me* away. Pushed me here to a party I don't want to be at to find a date for a bet I don't even care about winning anymore.

"Oh, hey, Becky-Ann!" Murph says, trying to sound so chill that I know he's into her. I look up and see two women coming toward us. One is dressed like a sexy French maid. The other is dressed as a sexy nurse. Their makeup is caked on so thick you could see it from the moon, and if I had to guess, it's probably not only like that on Halloween.

"Heeeeeey, Murphy," Becky-Ann, the one in the maid costume, coos, throwing her arms around my buddy. "Good to see ya!"

Murphy ends their hug but keeps one hand on her hip as he turns to introduce me. "This is my friend, Billy O'Sullivan."

"Oh, very nice. Becky-Ann." She offers her hand, and I take it.

"Nice to meet you." I don't even recognize my own voice.

"Well, this is *my* friend, Connie-Joy," Becky-Ann says.

Connie-Joy slinks over my way and offers her hand. "Wicked pleased to meet ya, Billy Sullivan."

"Likewise," I say. I don't care enough to correct her about my surname.

"You look good, Murph. I like the fireman outfit. Very sexy," Becky-Ann says, eyeing him up and down.

"Not so bad yourself there, Becky-Ann. I got a knob that needs polishin' latah," Murph says, his body so close to hers that I don't think it'll be that much later.

"Your costume looks good too," Connie-Joy says, not meaning a word of it. I can tell she's confused. "Is that...a butt on your forehead?"

"No, it's a lightning scar," Murphy answers, at the same time I say, "Yeah. It is."

"He's Harry Potter," Murph says, staring daggers at me.

"Oh. Cool." Connie-Joy says, still not meaning a word of it.

I can feel everyone expecting me to comment on Connie-Joy's costume. I clear my throat. "You look great too. Good choice going with the fun nurse costume. The sexy one. Not like a real nurse's uniform where you're prepared to lift a patient who can't walk. Where you have to change their bedpan. Can't do that in a skirt that short. Where you have to be mentally and physically strong enough to help people pass away as peacefully as they can."

There's no way a space as loud as this should feel this silent. But it does.

"Thank you," Connie-Joy says, continuing her streak of not meaning any of the words that come out of her mouth.

Murph looks at me and mutters, "What the fuck, Billy?"

I shake my head. "Sorry."

Murphy claps his hands. "We need drinks. What do you say, Becky-Ann? Should we retrieve some libations?"

Becky-Ann curtsies and, in a terrible French accent, says, "Wee, sir. Whatevah you say, sir."

Murph smiles and offers his arm, which Becky-Ann takes. They walk off together toward the bar, and he throws me a thumbs-up.

I turn back to Connie-Joy. She looks at me expectantly. I guess I should make conversation. "So, what do you do in real life?"

"Oh, I'm in finance," she says.

I nod. "Nice."

She shrugs, clearly disagreeing but not wanting to say so. "I guess."

"You don't like it?"

"Not really. But the money's good."

"I see. So what do you do with the money?"

"I...go on vacation. Save it in my 401(k)."

"So you can get away from your job someday?"

She looks at me like that should be obvious. "Yeah, that's what most people do."

"You're not wrong about that," I mutter. I look around the party. People wearing costumes so they don't have to be who they are in their normal life. The normal life they don't really enjoy. Drinking alcohol so they don't feel like they normally feel.

That's never been me. I didn't drink to get away. I drank because it was fun. But so was not drinking. I didn't do or wear or say crazy things to get away from who I was. I liked who I was. That was me *being* who I was.

But I'm not sure I like who I am now. Did Donna change me? Why am I not fun anymore? Why am I the saddest fucking-sexy wizard who ever lived?

Donna didn't change me.

I changed me.

I realize it wasn't the partying or the whimsy that made me Billy Boston. I wasn't mysterious to people because of that. That was all window dressing.

The real reason people couldn't understand me is that I do what I want to do when I want to do it for as many seconds of my life as I can. When I want to take care of my cousin's wife's niece, I do. When I want to go to Iceland, I do. When I want to have an epic night of debauchery and wake up in a place I don't recognize, that's what I do.

But I haven't been doing that lately. Because for

the first time in my life, I have something that I don't want to lose.

We made this no strings because she needed an escape and I wanted to have fun. Hell, we were so serious about not making it serious that we weren't even us half the time. We pretended to be other people so that Donna never fell for Billy and Billy never fell for Donna. I know that's what she wanted in the beginning and what I agreed to. But I've been using it as an excuse.

Donna hasn't asked me to change anything about myself or to be someone else. She's been with me every step of the way. I stopped doing what I wanted to do and saying what I wanted to say.

Because I've been a coward.

I wanted to say that I love her. That she's everything I want in a person. She's fully herself too, and maybe we could be even more of who we are together —near infinite in the love and life and happiness that we could create as a team.

But I'm losing it because I'm not willing to be who I am, to go after what I want. I can't pretend anymore. I can't play the role of the guy who still has nothing to lose. I have everything to lose—the most amazing person I have ever met in my life.

I'm done pretending that I don't feel the way that I feel.

Who I am, deep in my core, who I've come to be in

these last few months, is a guy who's desperately in love with Donna. Who needs her more than he needs air.

I'm in love with Donna Fischer. And she's going to know it.

And maybe, just maybe, if she feels the same way, if she doesn't get scared and run, I have everything to gain too.

I don't want to party tonight. I don't want to wake up in some strange new place with a new person.

I want *my* person.

I want her to want me.

I want strings.

It's time for Billy to be Billy.

It's time to do what I want to do when I want to do it.

Murph and Becky-Ann return with drinks.

"I gotta bounce," I say to Murph.

"What? Already?"

"It was very nice meeting both of you. But I don't want to be here anymore, so I'm not going to be." I don't say it in a cruel way. It's just a fact.

"Nice meeting you," Connie-Joy says, not meaning a single drop of it. That's the Connie-Joy I barely know!

I clap hands with Murph. "Have a fantastic night, brotha."

"You too. Where are you goin'?" he calls to me as I walk away.

"I gotta see a girl about some candy!" I yell over my shoulder.

"Aww, hell yeah, dude!" I hear Murph say, completely misinterpreting that I mean actual candy. But I appreciate the positive vibes anyway.

I just might need them.

donna

"Trick or treat!" a little girl, probably around seven years old, shouts at me, holding a pillowcase open. I guess she's starting at the top floor of our building and working her way down because there isn't a lot of candy in that pillowcase yet. Her parents are standing about twenty feet away, down the hall. She's so excited to be on this free junk food-gathering journey, I could just cry.

Enjoy this special time in your life, little girl. Memento mori. Enjoy the transient nature of these earthly pleasures, for one day we will die!

"Well, hello there! Happy Halloween!" I say to her, perhaps a tad too enthusiastically. I am genuinely excited to be alive and not working on Halloween night and definitely not overcompensating for being dead inside because Billy actually went to the Halloween party that I told him to go to.

Chelsea holds up the big bowl of candy for me to grab a handful and leans in to mutter, "Take it down a notch, champ. You're scarin' the kids." She's here because her husband is on a business trip and she didn't want to be at her house alone. And because I sounded so morose when she called me this afternoon that she didn't want *me* to be alone. She was wearing a pointy witch hat earlier, but it made her scalp itchy so now she just looks like a woman in a black cardigan.

"Are you supposed to be Ginny Weasley?" the trick-or-treater asks me as I drop three fun-size chocolate bars and a bag of chips into her pillowcase.

I choose not to take offense at the "supposed to be" part of the question, as I am fully aware that I just look like a redhead in a sexy schoolgirl costume that barely fits anymore. This was from five years ago, which was the last time I had Halloween off. I was half hoping that Billy would somehow see me in it on his way out, get such a huge boner he wouldn't fit out the door, and have to stay to give out candy with me. But without the boner, of course. Because I would have taken care of it for him. But that is not how this night is progressing.

"I sure am! And I'm not even wearing a wig. You are such a pretty Barbie!" I tell the girl.

"I'm Elle Woods," she informs me. "From an old

movie called *Legally Blonde* that my mom always watches."

This revelation leads Chelsea to demonstrate the Bend and Snap, and it leads me to want to lock the door, eat the rest of the candy, plus some apple strudels, and then cry myself to sleep because Reese Witherspoon played Elle Woods and that reminds me of *Fear*, which reminds me of Billy railing me at the house that time and how he'll probably be railing someone else tonight.

But it's fine. "We're all gonna die anyway."

Chelsea and the little girl and her parents all stare at me.

"Oh shit, did I say that out loud?" I cover my mouth. "Shit. Sorry!" I say to the girl and grimace at her parents, who look a lot cooler than they are, apparently, so maybe they shouldn't be living in Jamaica Plain because we swear here. "Nobody you know is going to die any time soon," I assure the little girl. "Have a fun night!"

"Okay, you're done." Chelsea pushes me back from the door and shuts it before I explain to the child that it is inevitable that everyone she knows *will* die eventually, so she shouldn't get too attached to anyone, especially not a boy who makes her feel really good in lots of different ways. "Why don't you just call him, huh? You're the one who told him to go to the party!"

"What's the point? We're all gonna—"

"If you say we're gonna die again, I swear to God, you will die by my hand tonight."

I smack my lips together. "I'm not gonna call him. He deserves to have a girlfriend who doesn't work twelve-hour shifts or have a haunted house that needs major renovation work."

"You are out of your friggin' mind," she says. "If I bought a haunted house that needed renovation work done, Joel would file for divorce in a heartbeat."

"That's not true."

"No, it's not, but my point is your guy was willing to help you fix up that house—he did a friggin' séance with you, okay?"

"Because he thought we were role-playing," I say, rolling my eyes.

"And he flew your grandparents in from Philly for a Tomcats game."

"That was really sweet. But he was just trying to impress me because I was his dating coach."

"Right. And he just offered to hand out candy to trick-or-treaters with you because—what? He wanted to practice being someone else's husband? Come on. You wanna talk about how short life is? It is way too short for you to act like a dumbass just because you were once engaged to a totally different guy who turned out to be a dumbass. Y'know?"

I groan. That was so harsh. "You're starting to make sense now, dammit."

"Just call Billy and stop being a dum-dum."

I pull out my phone to call him, but I find a text notification from Piper.

Piper: *Hey! It's Halloween and I just realized I never checked in with you about the ghost! LOL that was the first time I have ever said that to anyone! Did you end up using the Ouija board?! <ghost emoji> <jack-o'-lantern emoji>*

"OMG," I say to myself. This is the text I didn't even know I desperately needed.

Me: *Hey! Can U talk RN?*

I am mortified that I didn't just type out the words *you* and *right now*, but whatevs. And now I'm remembering that people her age don't like talking on the phone. And then I remember that people *my* age don't like talking on the phone either.

There's a knock at the door.

"I'll get it," Chelsea says.

"Thank you!"

Instead of replying to my text, Piper calls me. She is truly an extraordinary young person.

I answer immediately. "Piper!"

"Hey, what's up?"

"Nothing, hi, I just wanted to talk to you about the, uh..." I go into my bedroom and shut the door so the trick-or-treaters and their parents can't hear me talking about a ghost. "I just wanted to chat about the ghost."

"Did you contact it?!"

"Yes." I tell her everything I know about the ghost and what happened when we used the Ouija board and what happened yesterday. "It said *Tell him* on the mirror, Piper. I saw her write it."

"I totally believe you. Wow, that's so intense... Hang on one sec, okay?" I can hear her muffled voice talking to someone in the background. "Hey. I have to get back to the party because they're gonna play a slow-dance song, but it sounds to me like there's still something the ghost needs from you. They say that Halloween is when the veil between our world and the spirit world is lifted, so if you want to communicate with Lara, now would be a good time. But don't go without Billy. It sounds like she's pretty upset."

I don't have the heart to tell her that Billy's at a party without me.

"Yeah, for sure. I'll be fine."

"I hope that you and Lara can both get closure soon, Donna," she says earnestly. And then she gasps. "Oh my God, they're playing 'Can't Take My Eyes Off You' by Shawn Mendes. Gotta go—bye!"

And she hangs up.

I hope she gets to slow dance with a boy who has an amazing butt.

I open the bedroom door and hear Chelsea calling out to me. "Donna! Babe, you gotta come see these costumes—they're so good!"

I join Chelsea at the front door and say hi to the mom and little boy in the corridor. The mom is dressed as Harry Potter's white owl, Hedwig, and her son's costume is a sealed envelope from Hogwarts. They are, indeed, such good costumes.

But the Hogwarts owl post reminds me of something.

Lars once told me that while his wife was sick and dying there was a point where she couldn't talk anymore, but there was something she needed to tell him, so she wrote him a letter. He was too sad to read it and then he was too busy arranging the funeral. After the funeral he couldn't find it, and then later he thought maybe it got taken away with a piece of furniture when he sold a lot of the things that were in the house.

That must be it.

The letter must still be somewhere in the house.

I need to find that letter and take it to Lars's grave.

"I have to go," I say to Chelsea.

Hedwig and the Hogwarts mail give me the side-eye as they walk away.

"Your costumes are amazing!" I call out to the mom and her son. "They're so good they reminded me of something really important! Happy Halloween!"

"Wow, you are really bad at givin' out candy," Chelsea tells me.

I am. And I'm bad at no strings. And dating. And being a dating coach to the only person I have actually wanted to date for a very long time. And being honest about how I feel and what I want.

We're all gonna die someday. I guess I just have to believe that even after we do, it's not too late to tell the person you love how you feel.

billy

THE FALL OF THE HOUSE OF FISCHER

I'm driving as fast as I can down the highway to Donna's house, and I was halfway there before I remembered that I know a guy with a helicopter and that guy is me.

I had stopped at the apartment, thinking I'd find her there passing out candy and we could have a nice quiet chat about how she owns my heart and she can have it forever if she's in the mood for that. Instead I found her friend Chelsea there alone, telling me Donna was acting strange and rushed off, saying she had something important to take care of. I asked if it was for work. But Chelsea works with Donna, so she knew it wasn't that.

Which means the important thing that Donna had to take care of was not a person who is alive or dying. It involves someone who has long since passed, in a house that is not safe, even though I told her not to go back there. God forbid she should just listen to me! But whatever help she needs from me, I'm going to give it to her.

The closer I get to Middleborough, though, the worse the weather gets. The rain's coming down in billowing sheets, and I can barely see the road. So it's a toss-up at this point if it would have been faster or safer in a chopper. I just know that any amount of time it takes me to get to Donna is too fucking long.

My hands are sore from gripping the wheel by the time I arrive, and the wind is picking up. All the windows on the first and second floors are lit up, but the lights are flickering ominously. I know I have an adrenaline rush right now, but I swear it looks like there's some kind of eerie purple glow around the house. Like it's the house itself that's manifesting this storm.

But that's not possible.

Rushing up to the front porch, I burst through the doors. "Donna!" I call out over the calamity of wind and rain and thunder. No answer. At least not one that I can hear. I remove my robe and drop it to the floor so I can run faster. "Donna!"

I find her in the sunroom, on her hands and knees. The room is dimly lit by a flickering lamp. A flash of lightning illuminates her. "Donna—are you hurt?" I bend down to help her up.

She slowly rises up off the floor. "Billy?" She sounds so confused. "What are you doing here?"

Another flash of lightning and I can see her stressed-out-but-still-beautiful face more clearly. "I went back to help you. With the candy. But you were gone."

I'm about to continue, to tell her what I need to tell her, but she grips my arm and frantically explains, "I have to find the letter that Lara wrote to Lars! There's something she needed to tell him! We just need to find it! Then she'll be at peace. I know you don't believe me, but will you—"

"Anything you need, babe," I say. "Just tell me where to look."

We both jump at the clap of thunder. And then there's a friggin' tsunami of blood that crashes against the windows. Blood?! What the fuck?!

Donna screams and buries her face in my chest.

"Baby, it's okay—it's just the cranberries." I have no fucking clue how it can be so windy that the cranberries are being blown out of the fucking bog that's, like, fifty fucking yards away, but this is happening.

"It's her! I don't know how, but it feels like she's angry and she's not going to stop until we find the letter!"

"I know, baby. I feel it too."

She looks up at me, so relieved. "You don't think I'm nuts?"

"I didn't say that, Red." I grin.

That makes her laugh, which makes *me* feel relieved.

The adrenaline easing up a little, I get a good look at her. All of her.

"Whoa. Hold up."

"What?" She seems worried by the way I'm eyeing her, like I'm going to tell her she's covered in blood or something.

"Are you wearin' a sexy Ginny Weasley costume?!"

She starts to roll her eyes at me, but then she notices what I'm wearing. "Are you sexy Harry Potter?!"

I give her a wink. "I solemnly swear that I am up to no good." But it's a short-lived break from the chaos. Now the shutters are banging against the siding all around the house. "We gotta get movin'."

"I remember Lars saying the letter might have gotten mixed up with things that were put in storage. I've looked everywhere, even the garage. Everywhere except..." She looks up through the skylight, toward the darkened top floor. "The attic."

Right on cue, there's thunder and lightning.

I grab her hand. "Come on."

We jog out to the front hall and up the stairwell. The lights are still flickering. The pipes are rattling inside the walls like the last time we were here. The walls are shaking and framed paintings fall to the floor. Donna pulls me toward the end of the hall. I tug on a chain to unlatch the panel to the attic hatch and then grab the pull-down ladder. I am a gentleman, so I let Donna go up first, hanging behind her in case she falls. The house seems to be collapsing around us, but I still have the wherewithal to check out her magnificent booty under that miniskirt. The knee-high socks and patent leather shoes are really a nice touch.

When we reach the attic, it's incredibly dark and the air is thick. It's like wading through a sea of angry black ink. The only light is from the flashes of lightning through the dormer windows to one side. I have no sense of how big the space is, but we can both stand up without ducking our heads.

I take out my cell phone and turn on the flashlight. With that I'm able to find a single bulb hanging from the ceiling in the middle of the unfinished room and tug on a string to switch it on. The attic is now illuminated with a soft yellow glow. Donna and I glance around the space. It's big. Impossibly cavernous. There are tons of wooden crates and a few dusty metal boxes and trunks.

"You start with that trunk and I start with this one?" Donna says, pointing.

"Sounds good."

I start searching through a big trunk and so does she.

"So...how was the party?" she asks out of nowhere

as she frantically rifles through things. Sounding casual, but there's something underneath it.

"Aw, it was a bust. Not really my scene."

Donna stops searching for a moment and looks over at me. "Since when?"

I shrug. I could tell her now, but I don't want to ask for forever when it feels like the world is ending. "I dunno." There's a cannon blast of thunder that's so powerful, the whole house shakes. I pretend I didn't hear or feel anything. "Why, did ya miss me?"

She shrugs. "Y'know. Chelsea is great company. But you're..."

"I'm what?"

She shakes her head. "I don't know."

The thunder cracks again, and the panel in the floor below slams shut. I don't even know how that's possible since you'd have to use a pole with a hook at the end to pull the folding ladder up.

"Shit," I mutter and walk over to it. "The door's stuck! I can't open it."

"What?"

The light bulb begins to flicker, and the house shakes from more thunder.

"Billy..." Donna moans. "I have a really bad feeling about this."

"It's okay, baby. We'll figure it out."

There's a huge roar of thunder. Donna shrieks and crashes into me. I grab hold of her. She's shaking so hard. That's when I realize how fucking cold it is in here.

Then all of a sudden a small wooden box tumbles off the top of a stack of crates and its contents spill out.

Papers fly everywhere, but a single envelope drops to the floor, separate from the rest.

Donna and I stare at each other, wide-eyed.

"Do you think…" I ask but don't finish.

Donna nods, leaves the safety of my arms, and goes to pick up the letter. "This is it. It says *For my darling Lars!*" She peers around like she's expecting something to happen now that she's found it, but if anything the storm only grows more furious outside.

"Read it out loud," I tell her.

As if in support of what I just said, the light bulb stops flickering so she can.

She goes to stand under the light, opens the letter, and clears her throat.

"'Lars, my love. There is so very much I want to say to you, and even if I had the strength to speak, there isn't enough time to say it. I wanted to spend the rest of my life with you, and I was so sure we would fill this house with love and laughter and children and grow old together. You know how much I hate to be wrong, but I hate being wrong about this the most.

I was so foolish.

It was only two years ago that I met you, but I think of that girl you met as such a silly young thing.

The fears I had. So scared of leaving the life I'd known, so frightened of giving my heart to you completely. I don't regret one minute that I spent with you, but I wish I had said yes immediately. I wish I had only ever said yes to you and rushed into your arms and never let go.

I hope you forgive me for making you wait.

I'll never forgive myself.

I miss you already, my love, and I'm so sorry for making you this sad. It's the opposite of what I want for you. It's the last thing I ever wanted for us.

But I still want this house to be filled with love and laughter and children, Lars.

I know it will be difficult for you and I don't want to let you go, but please promise me.

One day, promise me you'll find a good woman and fill this house with love and laughter and children.

I love you.

I love you.

I love you.

I loved you when my heart was strong, and I'll love you until after it beats the final time.

Thank you for loving me.

Forever your scarlet spitfire,

Lara.'"

Donna is weeping when she puts down the letter. She folds the paper up and slides it inside her bra for safekeeping. I take her into my arms again, rub her back, give her time. When she sniffles and wipes her eyes and looks up at me, I can practically see the words she wants to say to me on her quivering lips. I can absolutely feel them waiting to come out of mine.

But we just stare at each other and don't say anything. The light buzzes and then pops and the room goes dark. I'm starting to think the ghost or the house or whatever isn't happy with *us*, specifically... The house shakes. I hear groaning and the cracking of wood.

"Donna, get down!" I yell and pull her away from the sound, in the direction of the dormer windows. Just as we fall to the ground, a giant fucking tree crashes through the roof. I cover Donna's body with mine, shielding her from the debris.

When things finally stop crashing down around us, Donna cries out from under me. "Billy!"

"I'm fine! We have to get out of here!"

I stand up, coughing, and pull her up. I manage to open one of the windows. "We gotta climb out onto the roof—come on," I yell through the rain that is now pouring into the attic. I climb out first and then grab hold of Donna's hand and guide her out.

We steady ourselves, standing on the undamaged part of the roof. Both getting pelted by raindrops, looking around, my hand locked with hers. I'm not going to let her fall. But I don't think there's any way for us to get off this roof unless I call the fire department.

"How are we supposed to get down?" she asks.

I look around for a way out. There is none. And then it hits me. "Well, Donna...sometimes the only way down is through..."

She looks at me like I'm nuts. "Huh?!"

I carefully turn to face her and hold on to her shoulders. "What did the mirror say?"

Donna looks so confused. "Tell him."

"I don't think it was Lars you were supposed to tell. He already knew how much Lara loved him."

It's like the whole rooftop is lit up by Donna's bright eyes when it dawns on her what I'm talking about.

We both say at the same time, "I love you!"

She grabs my face. "I love you so much, Billy!"

"I love you so friggin' much, Donna Fischer. I'm so crazy in love with you, and I don't want anyone else. Just you. Only ever you. I've never been afraid of anything before, but I was so scared of scarin' you away. I'll do anything for you, and I want all the strings."

"Me too! I'm still scared, but I'm not afraid to tell you I love you anymore, because you deserve to know how happy you make me. I love you so much I'm willing to face the pain of losing you someday."

"Aw, you're never gonna lose me, baby. Not evah.

Now that I know I can haunt you from beyond the grave."

I kiss her.

It's the first kiss in a series of infinite kisses I'll be giving this woman over the course of our life and beyond.

We're standing on a roof in the middle of a storm, but I feel so solid about everything, nothing can ever knock me down again.

When our lips finally part, we realize the storm has suddenly lifted. And by that I mean it's like it never happened. Aside from the whole *uprooted tree in the roof* thing. The rain and the clouds have vanished, there's no wind, the moon is shining bright, and the pale silver light makes everything look totally magical and serene. "I love magic," I say quietly, in an admittedly not great Harry Potter impression.

Donna peers through the dormer window and into the attic. The light's on again. "It looks like the hatch door is open."

"Fuckin' A." I climb back inside and then help her through.

We check out the master bedroom and the rest of the house. It's so quiet. Inviting and cozy, even.

"I think she's really gone this time," Donna says.

"Yeah. It feels different."

"I hope they're together now."

"Me too."

We survey the damage. Aside from the roof and the attic, it's just the framed pictures that fell off the walls. But the damage to the roof and the attic is...extensive.

Donna sighs and laughs the resigned laugh of an exhausted homeowner. "Great. Now I'm gonna need a new roof too."

I put my arm around her. "Well, this might be a good time to tell you that I'm a multimillionaire."

Donna slowly turns to face me. "What?"

I shrug. "Yeah. I won the Massachusetts lottery before I won the hot-lady lottery and got into a no-strings thing with you, and now I'm kind of a big-deal investor and entrepreneur. So none of this is gonna be a problem. I'll hire the right people, and we'll fix it up."

Donna snakes her arms around my neck. "You're always going to be full of surprises, aren't you, Mouth?"

"You know it, Red. For the rest of our lives and after. Happy Halloween, baby," I say, grinning. "You sure know how to show a guy a good time."

She laughs. Dropping her head and chuckling quietly at first, her shoulders shaking. Then she throws her head back and I get to hear the most joyful laugh I've ever heard from her. The laugh of a hard-working woman who finally knows that she's won the heart of a man who will show her a good time until the end of all time.

EIGHTEEN

"What am I gonna do—*not* be right about everything?"

I'm not sure anyone has ever been more pleased to see my red hair than Declan Cannavale's ma.

"What can I say?" she says to Billy's ma, shrugging. "I know what I know. And I knew your boy would end up with a beautiful ginger. I'm so happy for both of you, even though my youngest lost a bet—no offense. Eddie isn't used to losing, but all my boys are good sports. Even when they have to wear shirts for the wrong team—no offense. I grew up here and live in Ohio now, so I know how it is."

"Oh, Mamie knows *everythin'* about *everything'*, just ask her." Billy's mom winks at me and gives her sister-in-law a friendly nudge. She lowers her voice before saying, "But I grew up a fan of the New York team that shall not be named, so I get it too."

We're talking football because once we'd all finished dinner and everyone had given their birthday toasts celebrating Billy's ninety-year-old grandma, Nolan and Eddie made an announcement acknowledging that they lost the bet. Then Nolan, Eddie, and Billy unbuttoned their shirts to reveal that they're wearing Philly Lightning jerseys underneath and put on Lightning ball caps. They endured a lot of boos and hissing from the Bostonians and New Yorkers in this Irish pub. And they did it in an act of solidarity, because Billy won the bet and because I won Billy.

Billy and I have only been officially dating for a couple of weeks, but already I feel so welcomed into this family's circle. It's like they're forming a big, loud, protective ring around me. A big, loud ring with a lot of great accents and some truly amazing butts. I can't say I blame Piper for checking out her sort-of uncles' derrieres, because *wow*. Their ancestors must have done a lot of squats.

Billy is across the room, talking to one of his nieces, when we lock eyes and smile at each other. He's the life of the party, talking to everyone at once, it seems, but he never forgets to check in with me. It's hard to believe there was a time when the only way we connected was with our genitals. I definitely can't believe I insisted on pretending we were other people when Billy O'Sullivan is more interesting than all of those characters combined. I'm so glad we finally gave up the ghost when it came to pretending we didn't want strings, so to speak.

So much happened in October that we just eased into everything November has to offer.

When we were at the house last weekend, waiting for a contractor to show up, I asked him if he'd want to live with me there once we fixed the place up. He said quietly, without hesitation, "I want to live with you everywhere, Donna. Especially here." And that was that.

On Halloween night, back at Billy's apartment, we'd both dreamed about a man and a woman living happily together on the farm. We'd assumed it was Lars and Lara. But once we were back at the house, I knew...it was us.

Next week there's a PR event with him for his business. Later this month, he'll fly with me to Philadelphia for Thanksgiving with my mom and grandparents. It doesn't make my job any less hard or the end of a patient's life less sad. But being with Billy reminds me how much more there is to living.

I hope we can do all the living on Olander Farm that the Olanders never got to do together.

"How you doin' over here?" Billy leans in from behind my chair and rubs my shoulders. "You need another drink?"

"I'm good, thanks." I tilt my chin up for a quick kiss. "How about you?"

"Maybe later. I'm gonna get up and give one more toast first." He gives me a little pat on the arm before going over to the little stage and picking up the microphone from the stand. But he forgot to take a glass up with him. "This thing on?" he says into the mic.

Everyone instinctively looks over to Nolan, expecting him to come back with something lovingly insulting, but he just puts his arm around his wife, Cora, and leans back in his chair.

Even I know how unusual that is.

"All right," Billy continues. "I trust you're all havin' a good night—especially you, Granny."

"Gettin' a little nervous now, though..." she says, grinning.

"You aren't the one who needs to be nervous," he says. "First of all, I may have made this party happen, as none of you have mentioned—which is fine—but none of us would be here if it weren't for you, Granny. You not only made us happen by marryin' Grandad and givin' birth to your fine offspring but by bein' the kind of wife and ma that inspires generations." He clears his throat. "As you all know, I was the last of us to be inspired in such a way..." He looks down at the floor, just as I feel everyone else in the room looking over and smiling at me. "But I'm plenty inspired now. So if you'll permit me to do this at your birthday celebration, it feels right to do this in front of all the people I love."

My heart is beating even faster than it did when I was running through a haunted house. Ma O'Sullivan and Ma Cannavale reach over to take my hands in theirs.

"Oh my Lord, it's happening," Mrs. O'Sullivan mutters. She punches her husband's arm. "I told you, Oscar! Didn't I tell you?"

Billy just grins at me from across the room and says into the microphone, like it's the most natural thing in the world, "Hey, Donna. You wanna get married? I know a guy who wants to marry you. It's me. I'm the guy." He places the microphone back on the stand and saunters over to me, smirking, his hands in his pockets.

My eyes are watering and my mouth is dry.

He gets down on one knee in front of me, and his mom squeals as he pulls a small crimson-red velvet box out of one pocket. "Will ya marry me, Donna Fischer?"

I nod with my entire body and heart and soul. "Yes. I would love to."

He looks so relieved. I can't believe it would ever occur to him that I'd say anything other than yes. He opens up the ring box, and in it is an absolutely stunning ruby-and-diamond engagement ring. It feels like my eyeballs are popping out of their sockets. I want that.

"Aunt Mamie," Billy says to Mrs. Cannavale, "my fiancée is gonna need her left hand back."

I think both of my hands have fallen asleep because these moms have been squeezing them so hard.

They both pat my hands before letting go.

Billy slides the gorgeous ring onto my ring finger, and as soon as it's on all the way, he stands up and pulls me to my feet, holding me in his arms. "I'm gonna marry you wicked hard, Red."

"Bring it, Mouth."

As we kiss, all the marvelous butts in the room get up out of their chairs, applauding and cheering for us.

epilogue – billy

DAWN OF THE WED

"What do you want, Nolan? I'm not doin' shots outside of my own wedding. Especially when, out of the kindness of my generous heart, there's an open bar."

"That's courtesy of your wallet, not yer heart. And we aren't doin' shots," my best man informs me, snapping his mouth shut before he calls me fuckface or shitbrain or simply *eejit*. Because it's my wedding and I didn't want him calling me names today, so I bet him that he couldn't get through one day without calling me something insulting.

Nolan has gathered me, Declan, and Eddie on the front porch. My beautiful wedding to Donna happened in the backyard of the farmhouse, where the reception is now in full swing. The adults are enjoying a variety of cranberry-based cocktails of my own design, courtesy of our very own cranberry bog. There's also Guinness and Irish whiskey—I'm not gonna start a riot on my own wedding night. There are also bottles of Sam Adams for my Boston bros, kept on ice in an open coffin next to the bar. The kiddies get a cranberry-and-orange-juice cocktail that comes out of a skull-shaped dispenser, Hogwarts pumpkin juice, and mugs of hot chocolate with ghost-shaped marsh-mallows. I'm paying Piper to keep an eye on the kids while she's here, so she gets her very own virgin cran-berry-peach-flavored mocktail. Surprisingly, she did not get the joke. Possibly because she was too busy checking out the bartender's and DJ's butts.

I have so much to be grateful for today. Most of all, for my stunning wife. But the weather is a very close second. You just never know what you're gonna get at the end of October in New England, but we really wanted an outdoor wedding on the farm. I wanted to get married immediately, of course, as soon as Donna said yes. Not necessarily because I thought she might change her mind, but because I wanted to be her husband ASAP. But we decided to wait a year, until Halloween, because it's the anniversary of us finally being honest with each other about how we feel and because we wanted to thank the people who really brought us together. Piper said that the spirit world is closest to the living one on Halloween.

We left two seats empty for Lars and Lara, which

most of our guests understood as a lovely gesture—except Murph complained that they were prime seats. Which was crazy because he was a groomsman, so he was standing with me and the rest of the guys, but he had a tone in his voice like he could scalp tickets for them and get a really good price.

But after we recited our own vows and Donna said her *I do*s and *I will*s and I said the same, clouds sailed past the setting sun, making the whole sky seem to flash. It was like Lars and Lara were winking at us. It was a nice moment that Donna and I could privately share, even though we were standing in front of all of our loved ones.

All of our loved ones and about fifty jack-o'-lanterns. Donna and Chelsea and my cousins' wives went a little nuts with the whole Union of Souls/Till Death Do Us Part/Halloween-themed wedding. The kids are wearing costumes, but the grown-ups were given eye masks and hats and wigs to choose from when they got here. Everything's decorated pumpkin-orange and black, with pops of cranberry-red and off-white—which is not the same as white—something most straight guys don't know until they're getting married. But I know it now!

Donna's wedding gown is the most stunning cranberry-red-and-black dress I have ever seen, and her bridesmaids are in black. I'm wearing a cranberry-red tux with a black tie, and my guys are wearing black with cranberry-red ties. Our wedding party and Donna and her dad walked down the black candle-lined aisle to a string quartet playing "Thriller." And by "walked" I mean they danced like Michael Jackson zombies. It was wicked amazing, and she totally surprised me with that. Mark's son held a ring box shaped like a tiny black coffin. Our priest is wearing a skeleton suit.

For the reception, Piper suggested getting custom-made tarot cards for the table number settings. There are bunches of flowers stuck in pumpkins that were grown in our very own pumpkin patch. Would my beautiful wife and her lovely bridesmaids scold me for saying the flowers were "stuck" in pumpkins? Yes, they would. But there are a bunch of flowers stuck in pumpkins in the middle of a bunch of tables... You get the picture.

But now we're out here on the front porch, me and my three closest cousins.

"The time for drinkin' will come," Nolan says—not menacingly so much as *significantly*. "Now is the time for reflection." He pulls four cigars out of his suit coat pocket and hands them out. "You're the last one, Billy. We've all been made honest men."

He infuses the lighting of each cigar with the same significance that he used to lace his words. First Declan's, then Eddie's, then his own, and then mine—lighting us up in the same order that our worlds were lit up by our women. We're silent during all of this, like it's a proper ceremony that he's performing.

Nolan blows several smoke rings into the cool fall air. "So, Billy. What did you learn?"

I take a puff on my cigar. "What do you mean?"

The boys share a look. Declan looks back at me. "What changed to make you marriable?"

I stare back blankly. "I'm not following."

"I think what we're asking is what deep truth you learned to make it possible that you could marry a woman as amazing as Donna."

I shrug. "I don't know."

Declan sighs. "For me, I realized that no one gets me or keeps me in line the way Maddie does. That I wanted her handing me cups of coffee and rolling her eyes at me for the rest of my life. But to get that, to earn that, I had to let go and open myself up. It was... problematic. But I did that because I knew she was the one."

"*Okaaayyy*," I say, drawing out the word because I know that story. I saw it happen. Well, I saw him get drunk and make a lot of phone calls anyway.

"Or like Birdie and me," Eddie adds, pointing his cigar for emphasis. "She was my best friend. And I wanted to protect that. But her big brain and those lips..." He shakes his head, still clearly a lovestruck fool. "I needed to risk the friendship to gain my soulmate. We wouldn't be working together on our new

Shakespeare-inspired musical about Eleanor Roosevelt titled *A Roosevelt By Any Other Name* if I hadn't been willing to take that risk."

We all groan and chuckle.

This guy.

"Am I gonna have to see that?" I'm pretty sure it's clear from my tone that I hope the answer is no.

Eddie rolls his eyes. "It's just something we're doing together for fun. But if we do actually get it produced, you should be so lucky."

Nolan huffs. "Billy, I had to arrange a Vegas heist with the likes of all of you to win my bride. I wouldn't, couldn't, have done that before Cora captured my heart and inspired me to do so. So what changed *in you* to realize that you had to marry Donna?"

"Ohhhhhh," I say, finally getting what they're after. They want to know how Billy turned from boy to man. From party animal to stable husband material. From man of the world to man of the house.

I shrug. "Nothing."

The boys all share an incredulous look.

"What do you mean, 'nothing'?" Declan asks.

"What I had to do was change nothing."

The boys look at me like my bespoke cranberry-red tux is made of horse shit.

"What are you talking about? You almost lost her," Eddie says, exasperated.

"Yeah, but the problem was that I wasn't being

myself *enough*. I say what I want and do what I want when I want. I wanted to love Donna. And I should have just done it. I'm so unrelentingly perfect the way I am, I just needed to realize it."

"Unbelievable," Declan mutters, taking a puff of his cigar. "You can't even express a logical idea without sounding like a maniac."

I shrug. "I'm a simple man, fellas. I did what I wanted before I met Donna. I'm still doing the same. I do what I want to do. I just gotta keep doing that."

"Yeah. Donna," Eddie says, and the boys laugh.

"Yeah. Absolutely. I wanna do Donna. Forevah and evah. But also, she doesn't make things any more complicated. She still makes it simple. She loves who I am. And everything I do, I do for her. Not complicated at all."

They look happy for me. They really do. These guys that I've grown up and partied and adventured with. The fucks also look a little pissed that this all seems so easy for me.

"Well, wait until the kids come along. Won't be so easy then, Billy boy," Nolan says. "You'll see."

I shrug again. Mostly just to piss them off. Because while I'm longing to put a baby in the most beautiful woman on Earth, yeah, that is the one adventure that kind of makes me pause.

"I should have known," I hear someone say from the doorway. I turn and find my beautiful wife. My

271

wife, still radiant in her wedding gown but now pleasantly flushed from dancing. "Already stealing my husband away?" Donna smiles brightly, clearly enjoying the word *husband* the way I'm enjoying the word *wife*.

"Sorry, love," Nolan says. "We were trying to talk some sense into this...handsome young man."

"He is way too calm," Declan says. "It's problematic."

"He should be pinching himself for being able to marry a woman like you," Eddie adds. "He's a little too high on his own supply. He thinks he can just keep floating through life, doing what he wants when he wants. This is not ideal."

Donna holds her hand out, and I take it, helping her to gracefully join us on the porch. The boys aren't wrong about that part. I can't believe I scored a woman like her. But they're wrong about the rest. Everything comes up Billy in the end, so why would I change?

"It's all part of his charm," she says, offering her lips to kiss, which I gladly do.

When the kiss breaks, I turn smugly to the boys. "See?"

"We were saying *wait until he has kids*," Declan says.

"Then we'll see if it's so free and easy for Old Billy Middleborough here," Nolan says.

"That's a good point." Donna nods, getting a faraway look on her face. "Well, I wasn't planning on breaking the news here and now, but..." She places her hands on her belly.

My jaw drops. *No. Already? Am I ready for this?*

"Are you okay, honey?" Donna asks. "You look a little pale."

"You... We're... You're...?" I sputter. I'm going to be a dad. I found a girl who likes that I do what I want when I want, who does what she wants when she wants—when she's not working. You can't do that with a kid. You have to give them what *they* want when *they* want it. They get to drink and throw up and take naps in the middle of the day and not know where they wake up and play all day. It's totally normal for an infant to wake up in Michigan without knowing how they got there. That won't be *my* thing anymore.

Holy shit.

I scan the guys. They look just as shocked as me.

Donna throws her head back and cackle-laughs. "Trick!" she says gleefully. "Since you didn't give me a treat."

I squint my eyes, confused. "Wait, so you're not...?"

She shakes her head. "Not yet. You should have seen the look on your face." She grabs my cigar and takes a big puff.

Nolan, Delcan, and Eddie burst out laughing. Oh boy, do they think that was funny. Me, far less so.

"Well played, lass!" Nolan says.

"Welcome to the family," Eddie says, holding his arms out wide and giving her a big hug. A little too big, but I'll allow it, this once.

Declan is slow-clapping. "Perfectly executed, Mrs. O'Sullivan."

"We'll give you two lovebirds a moment. See ya back at the party," Nolan says, still shaking his head and laughing. They pat me on the back, go down the front steps, and around to the backyard.

Donna squints one eye dramatically. "Billy Boston-Middleborough, do you not want kids with me?"

We do still have my apartment in Jamaica Plain, so we are technically Mr. and Mrs. Billy Boston-hyphen-Middleborough.

I shake my head. "No, Mrs. Boston-Middleborough. I want to fill you full of babies more than anything. But I'm not used to wanting things this badly." I look around and lower my voice a little, not wanting the boys to hear about my actual doubts. "I wanted you so badly I nearly screwed it up."

Donna puts the cigar back into my mouth and snakes her arms around my neck. "Well, you did get me, Billy. And I'm nervous about kids too. But there's no adventure we can't handle together."

"You're damn right about that, Red."

"Come on, Mouth. We need to get back to the reception. You got your trick, now you need a treat."

"What is it?"

"Well, even if I *were* preggers, I'd still want to dance with my husband." She grins. "Because I will get knocked up, but we'll get down again. You're forever going to keep me now..."

On cue, the first bars of the greatest song ever, Chumbawamba's "Tubthumping," floats through the crisp autumn air from the speakers behind the house. My smirk is back in full force, and I grab my surprising, gorgeous wife's hand, ready for whatever adventure comes next. Our party's just getting started.

the end

about kayley and connor

Listen to Connor Crais co-narrate A Very No Strings Halloween, *as well as the other books in the Very Holiday series, on Audible.*

USA Today bestselling author Kayley Loring and narrator/Amazon Top 100 bestselling author Connor Crais have co-authored the Beacon Harbor series, the Boston Tomcats series, *A Very Vegas St. Patrick's Day* and *A Very No Strings Halloween.*

For more about Kayley and her books,
visit kayleyloring.com.

For more about Connor, his voice, and his books,
visit connorcrais.com.